CLUELESS McGEE

and the Inflatable Pants

Jeff Mack

PHILOMEL BOOKS

An Imprint of Penguin Group (USA) Inc.

FOR MY MOM AND DAD BECAUSE THEY
ARE BOTH REALLY, REALLY AWESOME.

Also by
Jeff Mack:
Clueless
McGee

PHILOMEL BOOKS
An imprint of Penguin Young Readers Group. Published by The Penguin Group.
Penguin Group (USA) Inc., 375 Hudson Street, New York, NY 10014, USA.
Penguin Group (Canada), 90 Eglinton Avenue East, Suite 700, Toronto,
Ontario M4P 2Y3, Canada (a division of Pearson Penguin Canada Inc.).
Penguin Books Ltd, 80 Strand, London WC2R ORL, England.
Penguin Ireland, 25 St. Stephen's Green, Dublin 2, Ireland (a division of Penguin Books Ltd).
Penguin Group (Australia), 707 Collins Street, Melbourne, Victoria 3008, Australia
(a division of Pearson Australia Group Pty Ltd).
Penguin Books India Pvt Ltd, 11 Community Centre, Panchsheel Park, New Delhi–110 017, India.
Penguin Group (NZ), 67 Apollo Drive, Rosedale, Auckland 0632, New Zealand
(a division of Pearson New Zealand Ltd).
Penguin Books South Africa, Rosebank Office Park, 181 Jan Smuts Avenue,
Parktown North 2193, South Africa.
Penguin China, B7 Jiaming Center, 27 East Third Ring Road North,
Chaoyang District, Beijing 100020, China.
Penguin Books Ltd, Registered Offices: 80 Strand, London WC2R ORL, England.

Copyright © 2013 by Jeff Mack.

Published simultaneously in Canada. Printed in the United States of America.

Edited by Michael Green. Design by Semadar Megged.
The illustrations are rendered in pencil on paper.

Library of Congress Cataloging-in-Publication Data
Mack, Jeff. Clueless McGee and the inflatable pants / Jeff Mack. p. cm.—(Clueless
McGee ; 2) Summary: Fifth-grader PJ "Clueless" McGee writes a series of letters to his
father, who he believes is a private investigator, telling of his attempt to learn who stole the
science fair trophy, thus clearing his own name. [1. Behavior—Fiction. 2. Schools—Fiction.
3. Private investigators—Fiction. 4. Family life—Fiction. 5. Robbers and outlaws—Fiction.
6. Letters—Fiction. 7. Humorous stories.] I. Title. PZ7.M18973Cmi 2013
[Fic]—dc23 2012035569 ISBN 978-0-399-25750-6 10 9 8 7 6 5 4 3 2 1

ALWAYS LEARNING   PEARSON

Chapter One
The Rocket Science Letter

MONDAY, APRIL 22

Dear Dad,

Thanks for the postcard. I can't believe you moved to Nashville! How did the bad guys find your hideout this time?

Well, you can relax now. Mom says there are no spies in Nashville hotels. Only "wannabe" country music stars.

I think it's safe to say no one will discover the **SECRET MISSION** there.

I hope you like your hotel. Last time me and Chloe stayed in one, Mom got mad because I was practicing my ninja moves on the bed.

Somehow the bed broke.

So just be careful if you guys do any flips or karate kicks in the room. They don't make hotel beds like they used to.

Not much has changed here since my last letter. Chloe is still a pain. She starts fights all the time, and Mom always blames me for it. I can't stand it!

Yesterday, Mom tried to show us how to bake bread. She said if the whole family learns to bake together, we'll be too busy to fight.

Only it didn't work because Chloe is a crybaby.

There were other problems too. Like deciding what kind of bread to make.

Finally, Mom exploded:

I GIVE UP, PJ! JUST PICK SOMETHING!

HOW ABOUT? PICKLE BREAD.

I'll bet you can guess what she said to that:

NO!

As you can see, Mom was being difficult. So I told her the same thing she tells Chloe whenever Chloe won't eat something new.

BUT YOU HAVEN'T EVEN TRIED IT YET. I'LL BET IT TASTES LIKE CANDY!

CANDY?

Mom just sighed and asked Chloe instead.

It's the first time that me and Chloe have ever agreed on anything! You'd think Mom would have been happy. But she wasn't.

I even offered to wear my ninja suit and chop the pickle with my bare hands. But she still said no. In the end, Mom made the bread all by herself. She didn't even try to cooperate!

Not only that, guess what she put in my lunch today?

I think Mom felt bad about it because she also put a pickle in there. I wish she had told me, though. When I unwrapped the tinfoil, the pickle flopped onto the floor and got hair all over it.

Just then I heard some yelling at the cheese-allergy table. Max and Jack B. were fighting as usual. So I put the pickle in my backpack and went over to stop them.

Ever since I rescued the mac and cheese at the Spring Fling concert, the kids here think I'm some kind of a superhero. As you know, saving the day can be a lot of work! But someone has to defeat the bad guys.

They're just lucky the principal was there to protect them.

Mr. Prince told me to save my ninja moves for Tae Kwon Do Club. That's what he calls it, but everyone knows it's really a secret club for ninjas! He's teaching the first class tomorrow. I just hope kids like Max and Jack B. don't sign up. They'd never survive one of my karate chops!

By the way, did you notice anything new about Mr. Prince? Check it out! He got **BRACES!**

I think it's pretty obvious why. If he's going to teach us moves for fighting bad guys, a set of sharp metal teeth is one of the best secret weapons a ninja could have.

Seriously, Dad! I can't wait to get my own braces! They would come in handy if I ever get to help you with the SECRET MISSION.

I gave Mr. Prince a few winks to show him that I had figured out his awesome plan.

For some reason, he didn't act very impressed.

He said I should sign up for an after-school club called Rocket Science. He said it might expand my mind. Yeah, right! As if my brain could actually get any bigger!

According to Mr. Prince, Rocket Science is really about learning, and making new friends. Plus, there's a big science fair at the end where everyone gets to show off their inventions.

I have to admit, I was a little curious.

Suddenly, I lost interest. As you know, a real private eye doesn't have time for silly stuff like science.

Then again, a real private eye never turns down a challenge.

At first I thought the prize would be something cool, like a billion dollars. But I was wrong. It was something even COOLER!

The winner gets their own official Rocket Science trophy! Here's what it looks like:

Pretty awesome, huh? It's probably not worth a billion dollars, but I'll bet it's close! It's made out of REAL metal!

Mr. Bellum is in charge of the Rocket Science Club. He also decides who wins the trophy.

MR. BELLUM →

CRAZY HAIR ←

ROUND GLASSES

MUSTACHE

BOW TIE

A ZILLION PENS!

WEIRD, OLD-FASHIONED CALCULATOR (NO TEXTING OR PHONE PLAN!)

You can probably tell he's a genius just by looking at this picture, huh?

His daughter, Sara, is in Rocket Science too. She's only kind of smart. Not a genius like him. See?

Just between you and me, I don't think it's fair that she can be in the science fair when Mr. Bellum is the judge. So I told her.

There's only one problem with that: She's not really the best! Today she built a tiny electromagnet out of some wire, a battery, and a metal bolt. But all it could do was pick up three paper clips.

I did one drawing and instantly came up with a WAY better idea! Behold!

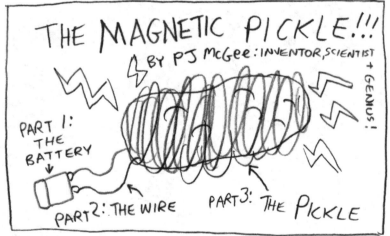

Sara says I copied her, but as you can see, my magnet is totally different!

First of all, it doesn't have a metal bolt. It has a pickle!

Second, mine has more wire. A LOT more!

And third, it's a bazillion times more powerful! As soon as I connected the battery, the pickle flew across the room and stuck to the Rocket Science trophy.

It was so powerful, it took five of us to pull it off. As soon as we did, Mr. Prince walked into the room.

HEY, KIDS! SHOW ME THE SCIENCE!

The pickle flew right out of our hands . . .

. . . and stuck to his new braces!

I think he was mad. But it was hard to tell because there was a pickle stuck in his mouth.

UH-OH.

Mm!! mmpH!

Not only that, he needed extra help getting the pickle off because his braces were so sharp.

Mr. Prince still seemed kind of angry afterward. But not me! I was just happy to get my invention back in one piece. I hid it in my backpack fast!

Think about it, Dad! This could be the best pickle ever for fighting bad guys! Especially if they use metal axes like in the SECRET MISSION.

And the best part: I invented it all by myself!

Love,

PJ

PS. When I was leaving, I saw Mr. Toots lock the Rocket Science trophy in the school display case using one of his million janitor keys. Something tells me he doesn't want anyone to touch it.

So I guess I'll have to wait until after I win the science fair!

Chapter Two
The Ninja Club Letter

Dear Dad,

Today was the first day of Ninja Club with Mr. Prince! I wanted to be ready, so I stayed up all night practicing my moves.

Only the strong survive Ninja Club. I figured I'd have to battle at least fifty kids.

But when I got to the gym, there was only one.

I almost quit right then. I can't battle Dante. It would be too easy! He's only in 3rd grade.

Luckily, Mr. Prince walked in with a kid I'd never met before.

GENTLEMEN, I'D LIKE YOU TO MEET BENNY. HE'LL BE SPARRING WITH US TODAY.

He was a lot older than Dante.

I'M IN 4TH GRADE.

He was bigger too. I could tell right away he probably knew a bunch of awesome ninja moves.

AT LAST, AN OPPONENT WORTHY OF MY SKILLS!

I was wrong.

This Benny kid should NOT be allowed in Ninja Club. I mean it! All he ever talks about is some stupid superhero named Captain Big Boy. He won't stop!

It makes me mad! Why can't anyone take this club seriously?

See what I mean? Ninja Club is a time for doing flips and kicks! Not for long boring lectures about school safety. But Mr. Prince gave one anyway.

Finally, Mr. Prince decided to teach something useful: how to block a karate chop from your enemy. He made me and Benny face each other on the mat.

I watched his hand. I watched it carefully.

I watched it go right up to his nose . . .

. . . and pick it!

Everyone knows I could defeat this kid with my little toe. But there was no way I was going to let him karate chop me with a booger on his finger!

Only one move could stop that!

Unfortunately, I ran away too fast and crashed into Mr. Prince.

Mr. Prince crashed into Mr. Toots.

And they both went sliding across the wet floor.

Mr. Toots did a complete flip . . .

. . . and landed right in his bucket.

SPLASH!

His keys went flying everywhere like a huge metal fountain!

I guess Mr. Prince was mad, because he made
me and Benny pick them up. All one million of them.

Let me tell you, Dad. Picking up a million keys
is exhausting work. And Mr. Toots didn't even say
thank you!

By the time we found them all, Ninja Club was
over.

I have to say, it wasn't the best class ever. But at least I didn't get a booger on me.

Meanwhile, Sara Bellum was waiting for me outside the gym. I could tell right away something was wrong.

Remember the rocket trophy that Mr. Toots put in the display case? You know, the awesome metal one that we both want?

Well, it turns out Sara can't win it after all! Since we were arguing during Rocket Science, Mr. Bellum talked to Mr. Prince about it. And Mr. Prince agreed with me! He decided because Sara's dad is the judge, she shouldn't be allowed in the contest!

She seemed sad, so I told her to look on the bright side.

How cool is that!
Mr. Bellum has a real laser beam! I wonder if he'll bring it with him to Rocket Science!

Even though Sara was mean to me, I'm glad I tried to cheer her up. Thanks to her, I'm going to learn how to shoot a real laser beam!

Plus, now that she got kicked out of the science fair, I'm definitely going to win that trophy! I just have to make sure no one steals my magnetic ninja pickle first. That's why I'm wearing my backpack on my front. As you can see, it's not easy to trick a private eye.

BY THE WAY, THERE'S A BOOGER ON YOUR BACK.

YEAH, RIGHT. NICE TRY!

Later, during silent reading, I did some serious thinking about Mr. Bellum and his laser beam. And I realized that Rocket Science is now my #1 favorite club. Think about it, Dad! Science can do amazing things! So while everyone else was busy reading books, I wrote a brand-new hit single about it.

It was impossible not to sing it out loud! So I did.

THIS IS CALLED "SCIENCE!"
BY PJ McGEE.

I LIKE SCIENCE.
IT IS RAD!
IT GIVES ME STUFF I WISH
I HAD.
LIKE ROCKET SHIPS THAT I
CAN FLY,
OR RAYS THAT SHOOT OUT
OF MY EYE,

A HAT THAT MAKES
ME SUPER-SMART,
THE POISON ON MY
NINJA DART,
A SMELLY BOMB! A SONIC BOOM!
A ROBOT MOM WHO
CLEANS MY ROOM,

A MAGIC DRINK
THAT MAKES ME
STRONG,
A TITLE FOR
THIS AWESOME
SONG.

Isn't that awesome?

Plus, it's all true.

Mrs. Sikes liked it so much, she said I could go to

the office and sing it

for Mr. Prince!

What an honor!

When I got there, Mr. Prince was already in the hall. So were Mr. Toots, Sara, and about six other kids. I was about to start singing when I noticed caution cones and yellow tape in front of the display case. It looked just like when the mac and cheese got stolen: a total crime scene.

Then it hit me: This WAS a total crime scene! Only it wasn't mac and cheese that was missing. It was the Rocket Science trophy!

Who would do something like this, Dad? Who?

Especially when everyone knows how much I love science! And how much I wanted to win that trophy! As usual, I stayed calm.

Mr. Prince tried to take over, but it was too late.

Mr. Toots looked for his key to the display case. But he couldn't find it anywhere!

Adults? HA! Somehow, Mr. Prince was forgetting one thing: I'm a professional!

Who rescued the missing mac and cheese? Me. Who saved the Spring Fling from total destruction? Me. Who's going to solve this crime too? PJ McGee, private eye! That's who!

Love,

PJ

PS. Now that I think about it, Dad, this should be the easiest case I've ever solved!

Chapter Three

The Captain Big Boy Letter

Dear Dad,

Help! Last night, Mom tried to throw away my magnetic pickle!

One thing I've learned: Mom is never happy about anything. First, she was mad that my backpack was full of gross stuff. Then, after I cleaned it out, she was mad that it wasn't!

Luckily, I was able to rescue my pickle from the trash can while she was making breakfast.

I guess it does smell a little weird, but I'm pretty sure nobody will notice.

It rained all day today. The school is leaking worse than ever! There used to be this big splat of mac and cheese on the cafeteria ceiling to protect us.

But now it's gone.

First, the ceiling started leaking. Then the whole roof caved in.

And now there's just a big hole.

For a while, Mr. Toots put buckets underneath to catch all the rain that poured in. But everyone kept tripping on them and slipping in the puddles.

So he finally went up on the roof and taped a huge piece of plastic over it.

That stopped the leaks, but now whenever it rains, it sounds like someone is playing the drums up there. It's so loud, we all have to yell just to hear each other. And that drives Mr. Prince crazy.

At lunch, I asked Dante if he had any clues about the Rocket Science trophy.

As usual, it was up to me to solve the mystery.

Here's what it looked like:

As you can see, the reward part was Dante's idea.

Me and Dante left our backpacks at the table and went to hang up the poster.

We hung it high so everyone could see it.

That was my idea!

When we got back, guess who was waiting
for us?

Something told me Benny wasn't going to be
much help.

I was about to say "forget it," but then I saw the back of his comic. It was covered with ads:

It was mostly a bunch of junk. But thanks to my incredible eye for detail, I spotted the only thing that wasn't a total rip-off:

THE X-RAY GLASSES!

These are glasses that will let me spy on bad guys right through a solid wall. Other than a magnetic pickle, or sharp braces, I can't think of a better weapon for private eyes!

I have to admit, it made me change my mind a little about Benny.

I picked up the comic to take a closer look. That's when I noticed something sticky and green right next to my pinky.

Mr. Prince got mad at me for yelling again, but I don't think it's fair, do you? If his pinky touched Benny's booger, I'll bet he'd scream too.

All I can say is, it's a good thing Benny had another copy I could borrow.

I grabbed it and ran out the door before another booger touched me.

Just as I passed the empty trophy case, I bumped into Sara.

We both went flying! So did our backpacks!

I tried to pick her backpack up for her, but I accidentally handed her the wrong one. I think she got the wrong idea.

I was shocked! Can you believe it? Me? A thief?

I had to find that trophy and catch the real thief fast! But how? During math, I read Benny's Captain Big Boy comic to get some ideas:

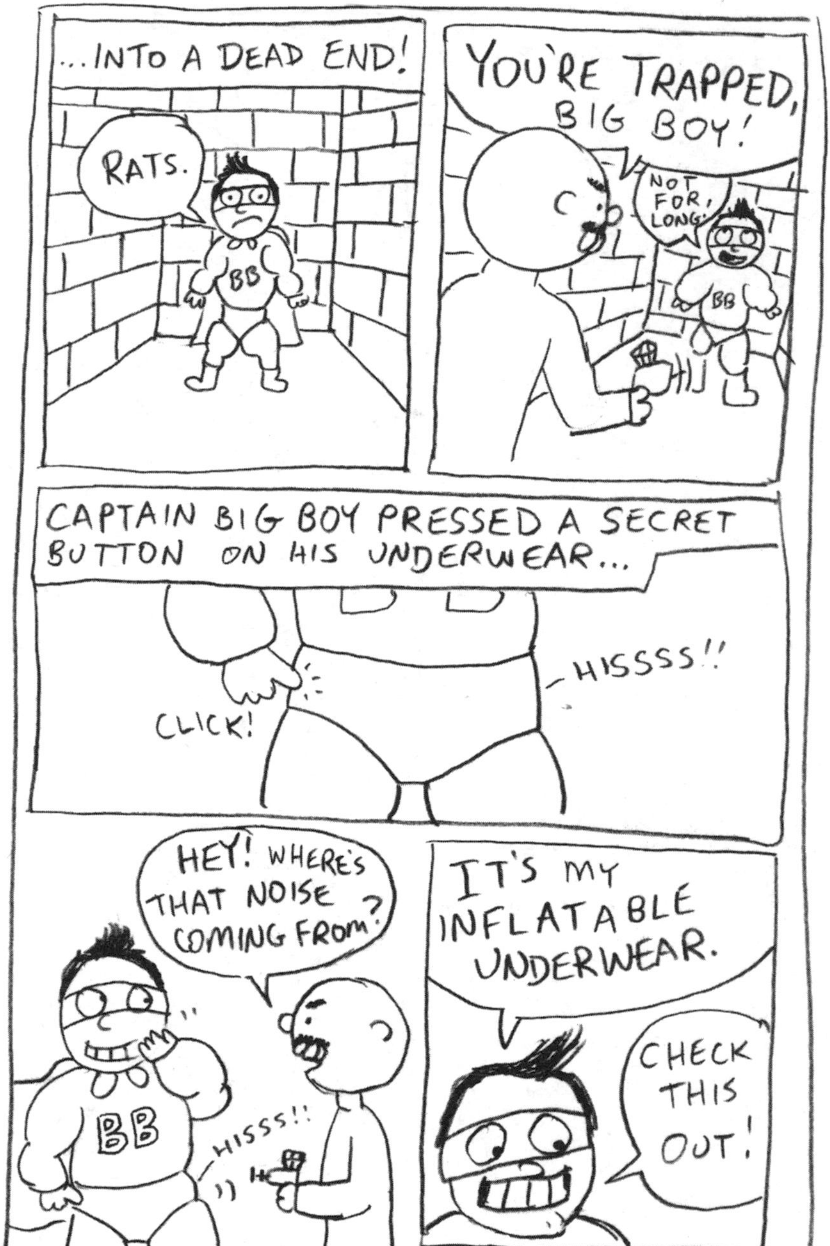
...INTO A DEAD END!
RATS.
BB
YOU'RE TRAPPED, BIG BOY!
NOT FOR LONG!
BB
CAPTAIN BIG BOY PRESSED A SECRET BUTTON ON HIS UNDERWEAR...
HISSSS!!
CLICK!
HEY! WHERE'S THAT NOISE COMING FROM?
BB
HISSS!!
IT'S MY INFLATABLE UNDERWEAR.
CHECK THIS OUT!

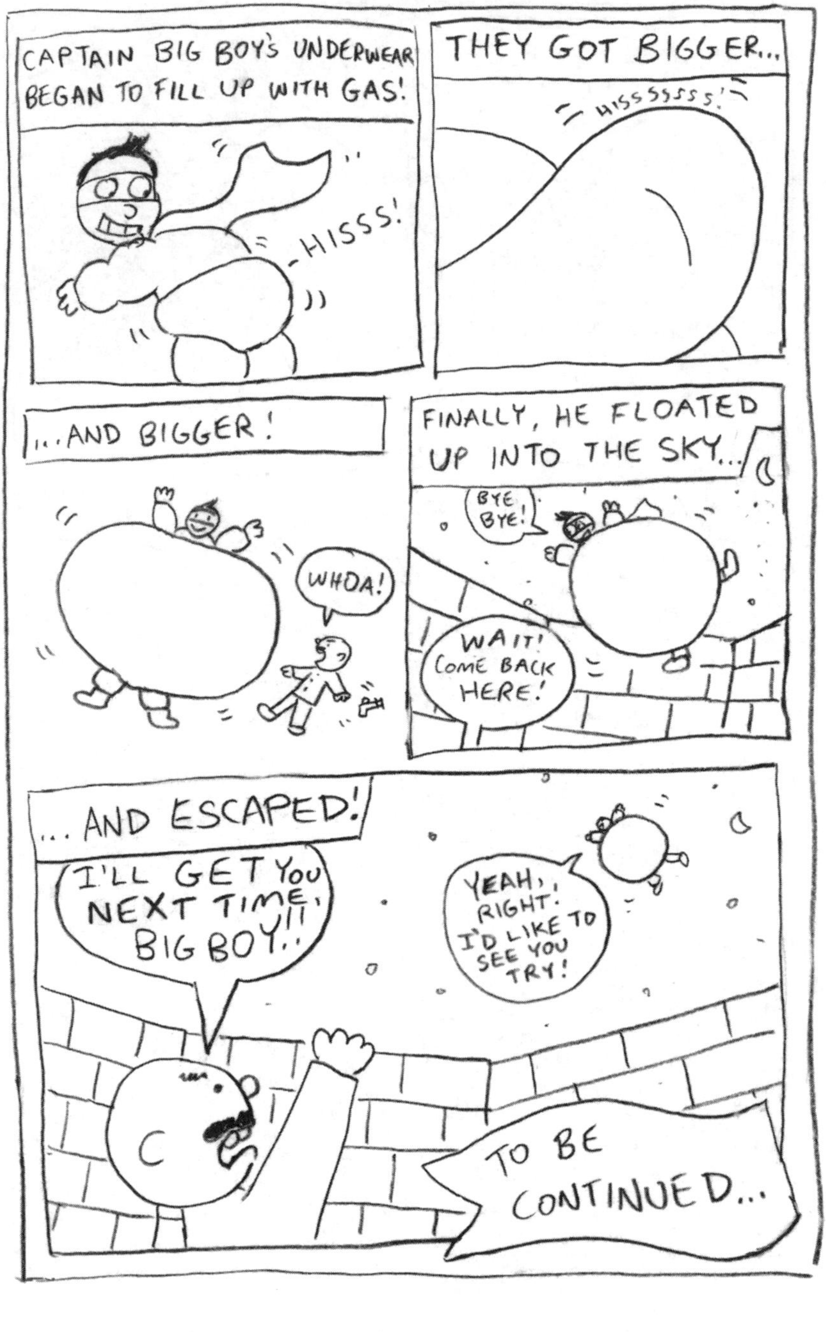
CAPTAIN BIG BOY'S UNDERWEAR BEGAN TO FILL UP WITH GAS!
HISSS!
THEY GOT BIGGER...
HISSSSSSSS!
...AND BIGGER!
WHOA!
FINALLY, HE FLOATED UP INTO THE SKY...
BYE BYE!
WAIT! COME BACK HERE!
...AND ESCAPED!
I'LL GET YOU NEXT TIME, BIG BOY!!
YEAH, RIGHT! I'D LIKE TO SEE YOU TRY!
TO BE CONTINUED...

It didn't solve the mystery, but it did give me an awesome idea for catching bad guys:

If only I had a pair of inflatable underwear like Captain Big Boy, everyone would definitely think I was a hero!

Mrs. Sikes made me sit at the tiny kindergarten desk next to hers. You know, the one she calls "the Hot Spot." She also made me put the comic in my backpack until the end of school.

Except when I opened it, I accidentally dumped everything out: my drawings, my songs, even my magnetic ninja pickle.

I was about to pick everything up when Mr. Toots burst into the room.

He was pointing to the pickle. There was something stuck to it. It was:

A KEY!

Mr. Toots and Mrs. Sikes started whispering to each other. Then they looked at me.

WHAT DID I DO?

They looked mad, but I didn't know why.

GO WITH MR. TOOTS, PJ.

BUT I STILL DON'T KNOW WHAT I DID!

Mr. Prince was waiting for us by the trophy case.

Mr. Toots
whispered
something.

Then he took the key

and put it in the lock.

It fit!

I heard a gasp and turned around. A whole
crowd of kids was
watching me.

I tried to explain, but Mr. Prince sent me to his office anyway.

As a professional, I like to stick to the facts. But I really have no idea how it got there. So I just named the first person I could think of.

Suddenly, I realized it was probably true! Sara must have hid the key in my backpack when we crashed into each other in the hall.

I'm pretty sure Mr. Prince didn't believe me.

He said I need to stop blaming others for my own bad decisions. But if you ask me, the only bad decision was kicking me out of the science fair! Plus, he let the real bad guy escape!

Meanwhile, everyone in school thinks I'm a thief! What am I going to do, Dad?

No one will ever hire me as a private eye around here again! I'm doomed! Doomed!

    Love,
    PJ

PS. Somehow Mom could tell I was worried, because all night she kept trying to cheer me up. Of course, it was no use.

Mom thinks buying new clothes is the answer to everything. Trust me, Dad. It's NOT!

As you can see, Mom knows nothing about how to cheer me up. That's why I can't tell her anything.

See through my problems? What was she talking about? Then it hit me: Maybe, for once, she was right. Maybe I just needed to SEE THROUGH my problems. Luckily, I knew exactly how to do that:

with a new pair of
X-RAY GLASSES!

There was no time to
delay, so I ordered
them online and chose
next-day delivery.

Luckily, Mom always keeps an emergency credit
card in her purse. And as you can see, this is a
serious emergency!

Once I get those
glasses, I can solve
this mystery. Then
I'll be a hero and
no one will ever call
me a thief again!

Chapter Four
The Inflatable Pants Letter

THURSDAY, APRIL 25

Dear Dad,

Mom made me wear my new pants to school today. They were so big on me, I had to hold on to them so they wouldn't fall down.

At first, I thought she might be right. Nobody noticed my huge pants or said anything about the trophy. It was like they all forgot. So I hung up a new poster just to make sure.

But when I turned around again, everyone was staring at me. It was like they all suddenly remembered.

Out of the whole school, there isn't a single kid who believes me.

Ok. There's one kid.

But Dante is only in 3rd grade. I needed help from someone much older and wiser. Someone who could tell me where to find a stolen rocket ship trophy.

I couldn't find anyone like that, so I asked Benny.

Can you believe it? Even though he's in 4th grade, Benny still believes Captain Big Boy is a real person like Captain Hook or Darth Vader. I guess I just don't have the heart to tell him the truth.

So as usual, I'll be solving this mystery on my own!

There was only one way to do it: I had to sneak into the science room and search for clues. But how?

That was probably the worst idea I've ever heard. Me? An assistant? Never!

Leave it to Dante to come up with a terrible idea like that.

Dante showed me a drawing he made of his own invention. He called it "space mail."

It was pretty much the worst idea ever.

Dante made me and Benny promise not to tell anyone his idea, even though it stunk.

Seriously, Dad. There's no way I was going to help Dante make a stupid space-mail balloon. Not when I could come up with something a bazillion times better.

I had to admit, for once Benny was on to something!

It was true! My pants were huge!

Suddenly, I knew what I had to do!

During silent reading, I drew my plan:

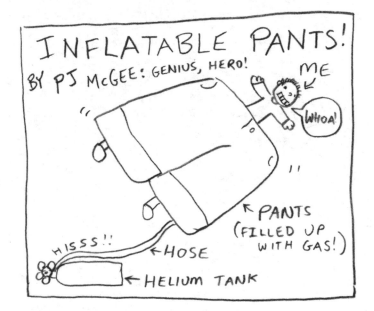

It came out incredible!

Let me tell you, Dad. It's not easy being a genius and a hero at the same time.

Especially when nobody lets you.

Later, when me and Dante got to Rocket Science, guess who we saw?

It was Sara! She was working on a volcano with Mr. Bellum.

Dante thought it looked cool, but I didn't. You could tell it was totally fake.

Even after she got disqualified, Sara still came to Rocket Science. She's got a lot of nerve, if you ask me.

I told Dante to get the helium ready for his space-mail invention while I spied on Sara for clues.

Thanks to him, my cover was totally blown!

Not only that, someone must have warned her about our secret plan.

I still don't know why Sara bothered to show up to Rocket Science when she knows she can't win the trophy.

If you ask me, Dad, this girl is clueless!

Just when Dante was about to connect the helium to his balloon, Sara's volcano started to erupt.

Gross pink slime started pouring out all over. Everyone ran over to watch.

Except for me. It was the perfect time to secretly test out my new invention. Before anyone could see, I stuck the hose up my pant leg and turned on the helium.

The erupting volcano was making so much noise, no one heard the hissing as my pants slowly filled up with gas.

I could feel my pants
stretch. They were like
a huge balloon . . .

. . . growing bigger . . .

HISSSSSS

HISSSSS

. . . and bigger!

I waited until my
pants were totally
filled with gas. Then
I tried to shut off the
tank. But I couldn't reach it!

UH-OH!

HISSSSS

Just then, Mr. Prince walked into the room.

And my pants exploded!

Pieces of pants went flying everywhere!

Mr. Prince was so scared, he crashed backward into Sara's fake volcano.

Gross pink slime splattered all over his suit. And his hand got stuck inside. I could tell he was mad, but it was Sara's fault for leaving her volcano there.

It's times like these when a little professional help comes in handy. So they were lucky I was there.

When we finally got the volcano off, Sara didn't even thank me.

Now that I think of it, Mr. Prince didn't thank me either. In fact, he said I was banned from the science room!

Luckily, the nurse gave me a towel to wear on the bus. When I got home, Mom didn't even notice that my new pants were gone. She was busy baking a pineapple upside-down cake with Chloe.

Don't ask me why they call it upside-down cake. It looked right side up to me.

On the bright side, guess what was waiting for me with the mail? My X-RAY GLASSES!

They are a little big on me. I think it's because they're meant for older private eyes like you.

I also think they're going to take some getting used to. I haven't been able to see through any walls yet. Right now everything just looks dark and blurry. But I'm sure that will get better with practice.

I'm definitely going to find the trophy with these!

Love,

PJ

PS. I just found out why it's called upside-down cake.

Chapter Five
The X-Ray Glasses Letter

FRIDAY, APRIL 26

Dear Dad,

Mom made me wear another huge pair of pants to school today. She says I outgrow my clothes too fast, so all the new pants she buys me are gigantic!

Not only that, she also said I wasn't allowed to wear my X-ray glasses to school. She says they're too dangerous. But it's actually just the opposite! I practiced with them all night, and now I can see even better with them on.

I had to get them to school somehow. So I hid them in a place Mom would never dare to look:

It was the only way!

When I got to school, I was sure I'd be the only private eye wearing cool X-ray glasses like these. But I was wrong.

I have to admit, for once Benny looked almost as cool as me. He seemed really excited to use his new X-ray powers, so I let him help me search for the missing trophy. We must have looked everywhere.

But it was no use.

On the bright side, even Benny says he can see better wearing the glasses.

So it must be true.

I SEE LONDON.
I SEE FRANCE.
I SEE PJ's
UNDERPANTS!

We had art class with Ms. Julian today. We're making shoebox dioramas. Just so you know, a diorama is an awesome scene made out of stuff you put in a shoebox. Except most kids' scenes aren't very awesome.

For example, Taylor M. is making a "My Precious Pony" scene.

And Taylor W. is making a "My Precious Baby" scene.

Ms. Julian always tries to think of nice things to say. Even for the bad ones.

My scene is a *ninja* hideout. And the best part is, all my *ninja* guys are made out of pickles!

The pickle in the middle is the ninja master. All the pickles around him are his students. And on the outside are the bad guys trying to defeat them. As you can see, I had to use a lot of tape.

I also used ketchup for blood. Taylor M. said it was gross, but Ms. Julian called it inventive!

Sara's in art too. She's pretty much the worst artist in the class. For her diorama, she made a science lab, but the only things in it are a test tube and a spoon.

SCIENCE

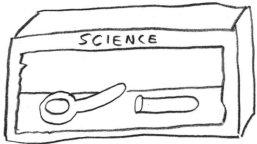

Ms. Julian said she liked it, but she was probably just pretending so she wouldn't hurt Sara's feelings.

IT LOOKS VERY SCIENTIFIC, SARA.
YOU'RE RIGHT! IT IS!

Once every class has finished their dioramas, Ms. Julian is going to set them up on display in the cafeteria.

The only problem is there's no prize for the best diorama. Ms. Julian says art shouldn't be a contest.

I think it's safe to say that everyone will like mine the best!

During lunch, Dante asked to borrow the back of my Captain Big Boy comic. I told him I already tore out the X-ray glasses ad, but he took it anyway. Who knows? Maybe he wants the whoopee cushion.

Then I told Dante and Benny how Sara stole the key to the trophy case and hid it in my backpack so I would get blamed. At first, it seemed like Dante was on my side.

Then it didn't.

It's times like these when you find out who your real friends are. So I asked Benny if Sara was innocent or guilty.

As you can see, Benny is a real friend. I told Dante if he ever hopes to be my partner, he should act more like Benny and help me get Sara in trouble.

For some reason, Dante got mad and left.

So me and Benny got to work on the new posters by ourselves. Here's what mine looked like:

Benny wore his X-ray glasses while he made his poster. He said they help him draw better. But I'd hate to see how he draws without them.

I went to hang the posters up while Benny stayed at the table and kept a lookout for bad guys.

Mrs. Sikes only let me hang one poster:
Benny's! It's not fair, Dad! My poster was way
better than his!

I could tell she didn't want to hear the truth.
So I took the poster down and went to get my
backpack.

We looked everywhere for Sara.

It wasn't easy, but we finally found her near the trophy case. Something told me the trophy was in her backpack.

This was my big chance! If it was in there, I could arrest her on the spot. I tried to use my X-ray glasses to see inside, but she was walking too fast.

I think she felt like she was being followed, because all of a sudden, she stopped.

So we crashed.

On the bright side, I finally found out what was in her backpack. Too bad it wasn't the trophy.

I decided to arrest her anyway.

As you know, Sara can be dangerous when she's mad.

Luckily, I had my new partner to protect me. Nothing scares Benny.

Well, almost nothing.

As you can see, there was only one thing left to do.

Benny ran one way.
I ran the other.

Unfortunately, I ran the wrong way.

As usual, everything fell out of my backpack! All my papers, poems, comic books, my magnetic pickle, and something else:

It was . . .

THE ROCKET SCIENCE TROPHY!

The trophy flew one way, my pickle flew another, and my papers flew everywhere!

Mr. Prince picked up the trophy and stared
at me. A huge crowd circled around us. Everyone
gasped.

I turned to look, but Sara was gone. Once
again, I had no proof.

Can you believe it, Dad? Me? A detention?
After all I've done for this school? What about
saving the Spring Fling? What about finding the
mac and cheese? Detentions are supposed to be
for bad kids. Not heroes like me.

How can Mr. Prince not see what happened?
Sara put the trophy in my backpack so that
everyone would think I stole it! It's so obvious!
Isn't it?

Now everyone really does think I stole the trophy!

As a fellow private eye, I think you'll agree there's only one professional thing to do in a situation like this:

Beg!

Love,
PJ

PS. Going to detention was probably the worst thing I've ever had to do.

Basically, I had to sit in the Hot Spot for almost an hour while Mrs. Sikes read a magazine!

It was torture!

I spent most of the time just thinking about you hiding out with the SECRET MISSION in a Nashville hotel. Just so you know, Dad, I think about you pretty much ALL THE TIME.

But I'm sure you think about me all the time too. Right?

Anyway, I still had Benny's Captain Big Boy comic with me. So when Mrs. Sikes wasn't looking, I read a few pages. Here's what happened:

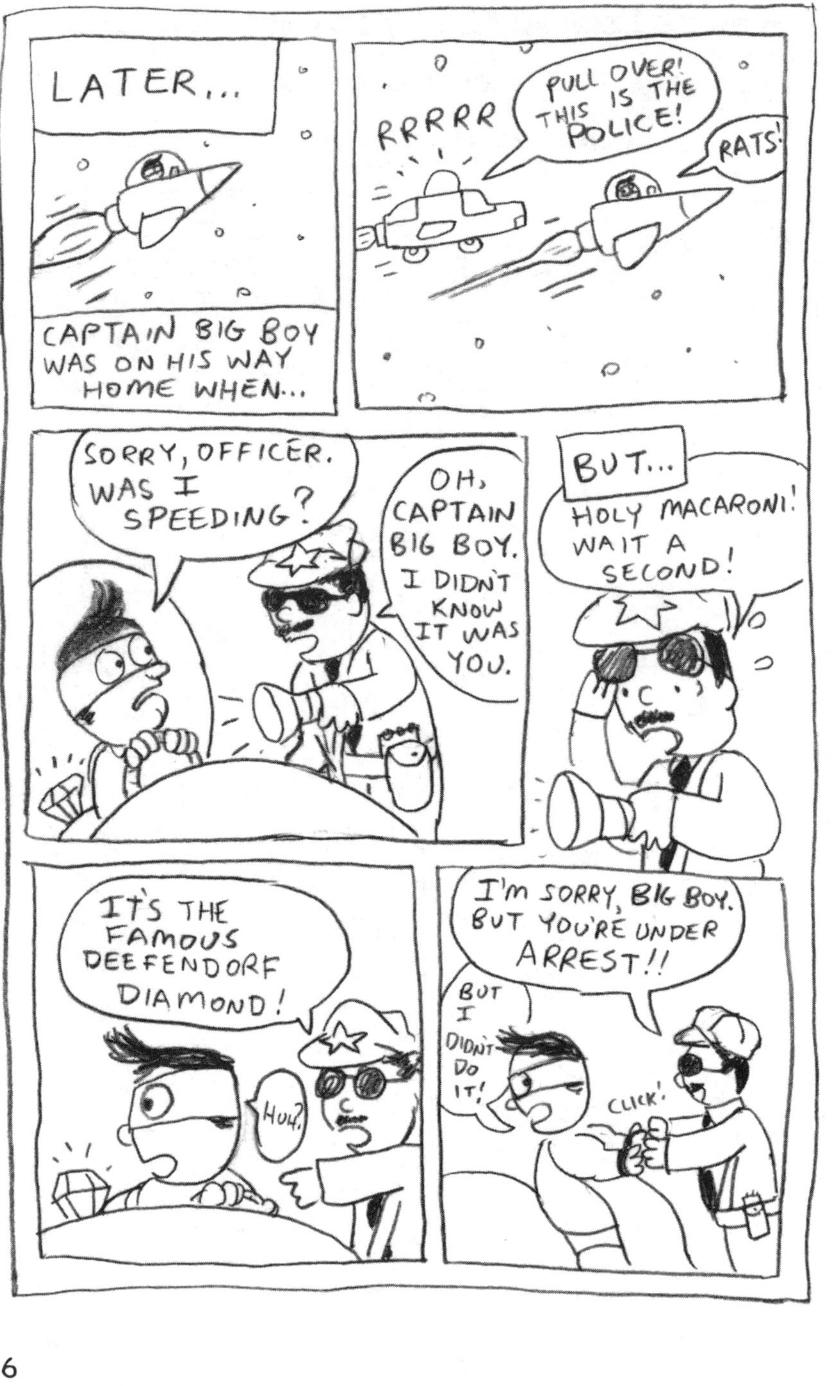
LATER...
CAPTAIN BIG BOY WAS ON HIS WAY HOME WHEN...
RRRRR
PULL OVER! THIS IS THE POLICE!
RATS!
BUT...
SORRY, OFFICER. WAS I SPEEDING?
OH, CAPTAIN BIG BOY. I DIDN'T KNOW IT WAS YOU.
HOLY MACARONI! WAIT A SECOND!
IT'S THE FAMOUS DEEFENDORF DIAMOND!
HUH?
I'M SORRY, BIG BOY. BUT YOU'RE UNDER ARREST!!
BUT I DIDN'T DO IT!
CLICK!

Did you see that? Captain Big Boy got in trouble for something he didn't even do!

I have to say, I know how he feels.

Chapter Six
The Baking Letter
(Part One)

SATURDAY, APRIL 27

Dear Dad,

Today was Saturday. As usual, Mom took a nap.
Can you believe it? Weekends are supposed to be
time for video games and practicing ninja moves.
Like these:

But all Mom wants to do is sleep. I don't get it. Why is she so tired all the time?

After about three hours of ninja moves, she told me I had to do something intelligent.

Let me tell you, reading to Chloe is a real pain. She always asks a bazillion silly questions. So I took the Captain Big Boy comic from my backpack and started to read the most boring part: the ads.

YOUR VERY OWN ROCKET SHIP. LOOKS LIKE REAL METAL. JUST LIKE CAPTAIN BIG BOY'S. AWESOME SECRET PRIZE INSIDE.

I figured she would get sick of it faster and go away.

A SECRET PRIZE? WOW!

I was wrong.

WHAT'S THE SECRET? IS IT ALIVE? IS IT A PONY? IS IT A UNICORN? WHAT DO I FEED IT?

I tried to tell her that you have to buy the rocket before you get the prize . . .

. . . but she wouldn't listen.

Finally, I couldn't take it anymore.

Luckily, that's when Mom asked Chloe to help her do some baking.

So I started reading the comic to myself. Just so you know, it was a really intelligent part:

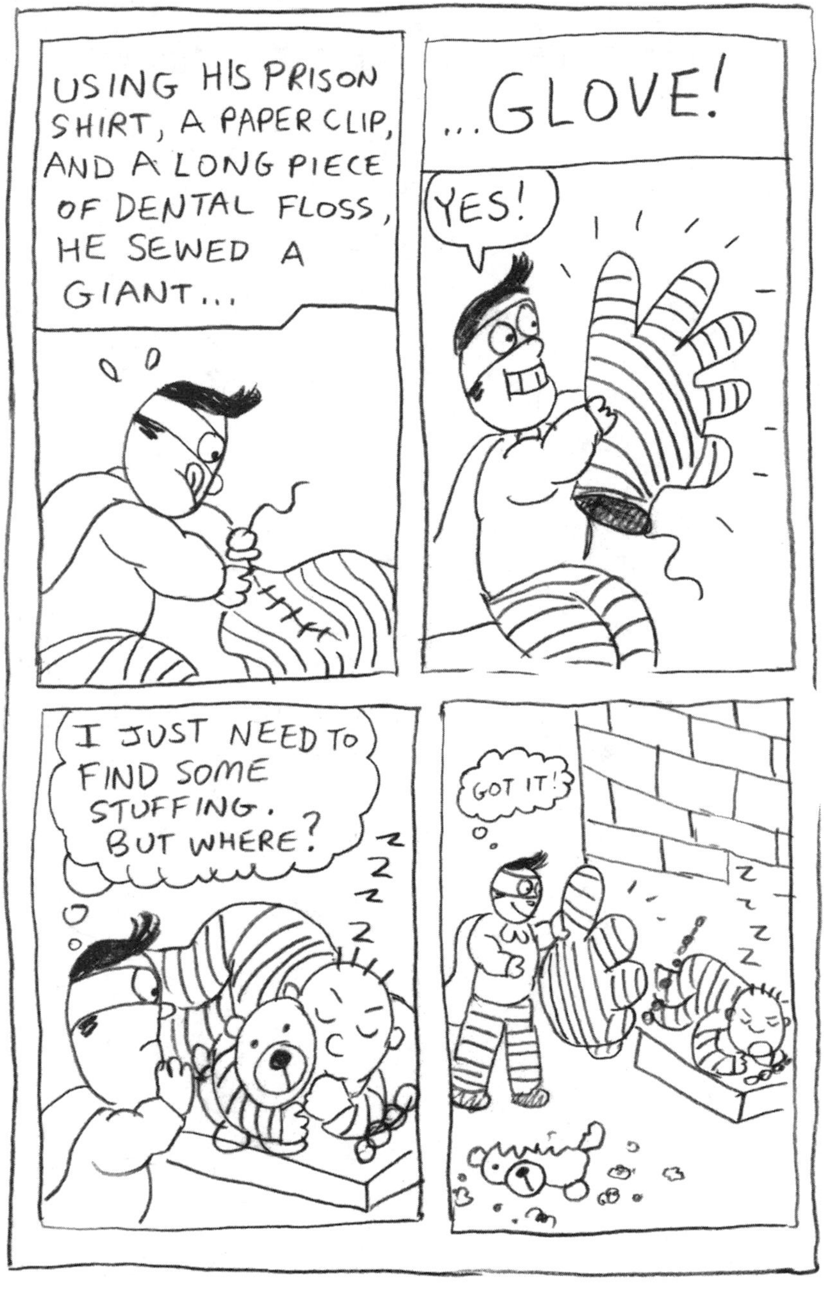
USING HIS PRISON SHIRT, A PAPER CLIP, AND A LONG PIECE OF DENTAL FLOSS, HE SEWED A GIANT...
...GLOVE!
YES!
I JUST NEED TO FIND SOME STUFFING. BUT WHERE?
Z
Z
Z
Z
GOT IT!
Z
Z
Z
Z

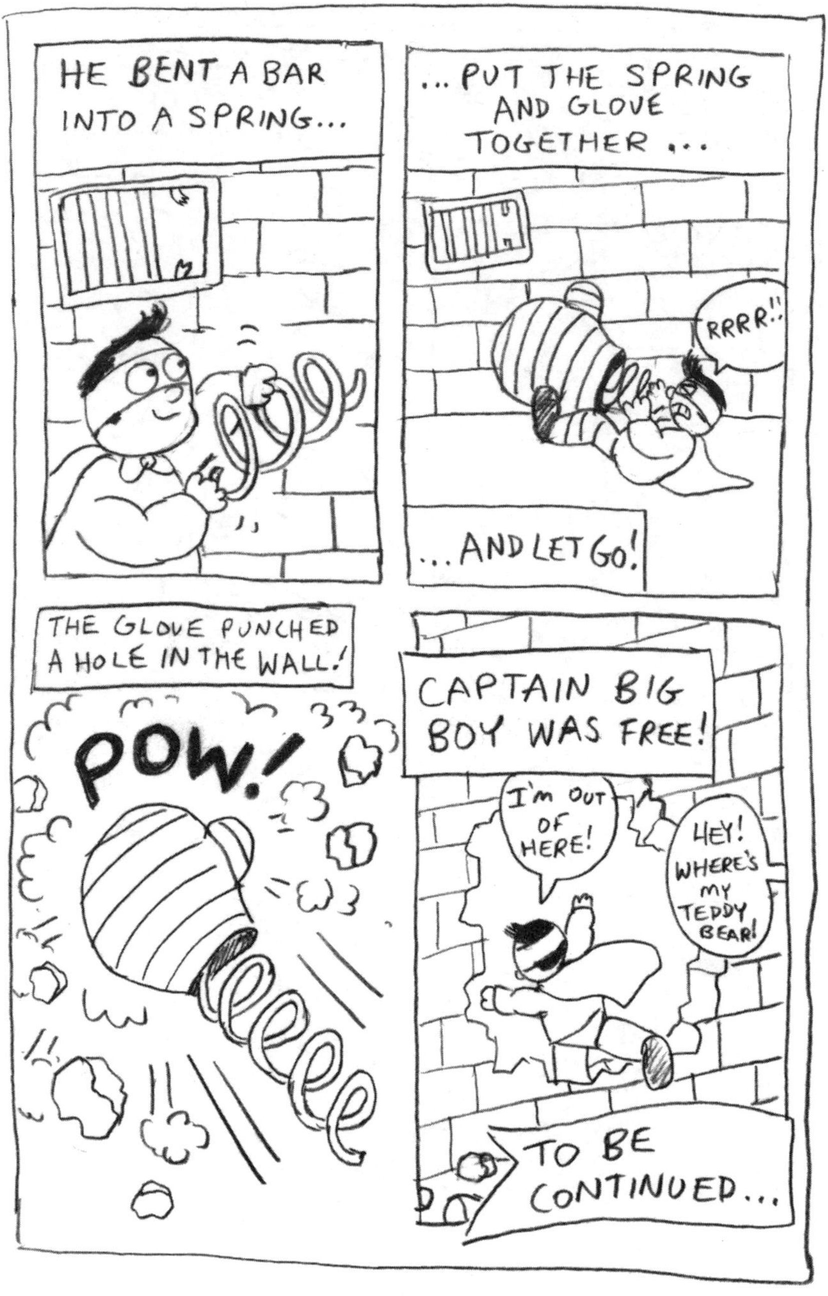
HE BENT A BAR INTO A SPRING...
...PUT THE SPRING AND GLOVE TOGETHER...
RRRR!!
...AND LET GO!
THE GLOVE PUNCHED A HOLE IN THE WALL!
POW!
CAPTAIN BIG BOY WAS FREE!
I'M OUT OF HERE!
HEY! WHERE'S MY TEDDY BEAR!
TO BE CONTINUED...

I'm glad I read it, because I got an awesome idea for a ninja weapon:

They make karate chopping a bazillion times more powerful.

They just take some practice first.

Mom said if I was going to goof off with her oven mitt, I could at least help her bake something. Yeah, right!

Mom said the first step was to add the flour.
She said there was only a little bit left, so we had
to be careful not to spill any.

As usual, I was careful . . .

. . . but Chloe wasn't!

So we ran out of flour!

Mom made everyone go to Food Giant to buy more.

As usual, pretty much half the school was there. But thanks to Chloe, we were the only ones covered in flour.

It figures.

PJ! I'M NOT GOING TO TELL YOU AGAIN! PUT THE CANDY BACK!

HE LOOKS LIKE A POWDERED DONUT!

Luckily, Mom remembered that we were also out of chocolate chips. So she also bought a bag of those. Well, two bags if you count the one that spilled.

It was a long ride home. But at least me and Chloe had a bag of chocolate chips to pass the time.

By the time we got home, most of the chocolate chips were gone. Trust me, I was as surprised as Mom.

So we had to go back to Food Giant for more chocolate chips.

It wasn't easy. Chloe asked to buy everything in the entire store.

Chloe doesn't like to be told "no." Like I said, she can be a real pain.

When we got home, we were out of sugar.

So Mom took another nap.

We never even got to make the cookies.

It figures.

Love,
PJ

PS. I forgot to tell you: Your package arrived today! Thanks for the awesome new hat!

Is this what private eyes wear in Nashville? As you can see, it looks totally professional.

I've needed a new hat ever since Mrs. Sikes took your trucker hat away from me.

I don't care what she says. I'm definitely wearing this one to school!

I also think it's cool that the SECRET MISSION is going to make a recording! Are you going to secretly record the bad guys over the phone or through the wall?

If you ask me, through the wall is probably best. That way you can hear them all talking at once. Plus, once you record them making an evil plan, you can use it to send them to jail!

Since you're going to be in Nashville for another week, maybe I can come out to help you. I'll bring my X-ray glasses so we can see the bad guys while you're secretly recording them through the wall.

By the way, Mom told me to say that Chloe likes her present too. It's the first fake talking parrot she's ever had. I think a bird that flaps its wings and repeats everything you say is almost as cool as a Nashville private eye hat.

I tried to help her set it up, but I think maybe it broke, because now it only says one thing.

Chapter Seven
The Baking Letter (Part Two)

SUNDAY, APRIL 28

Dear Dad,

I can't believe it! My Captain Big Boy comic has been stolen!

I've looked everywhere for it!

The first place I searched was Chloe's room.

Then I remembered something: Chloe can't read!

I tried to put all her stuff back before she found out. But it was too late.

After that, Mom made me clean up Chloe's room all by myself. It was really not fair!

As you know, Mom's idea of cleaning means throwing everything in the trash. So I thought maybe that's what happened to my comic!

Then, just as I was dumping out the trash, Chloe walked in. I thought for sure she was going to tell on me, but she didn't!

There was a lot of trash in there. And a lot of flour. But no comic!

After that, Mom made us go back to Food
Giant to buy more sugar.

Once was bad enough. But going there
covered in flour two days in a row is truly
humiliating. They must think we never take baths.

Just when it couldn't get any worse, guess who
we saw on aisle two?

I tried to duck behind a stack of cereal
boxes . . .

. . . but I slipped.

It was too late. Sara saw me.

When we got back home, I wanted to make the cookies again, but Mom had to give Chloe a bath. So she said I could measure two cups of the new sugar to get ready.

I got out the measuring cup and the bag of sugar. I poured it over the sink in case a little spilled.

It's a good thing I did. Because it spilled.

Pretty much all the sugar went right down the drain. But at least it didn't go all over the floor!

I didn't want Mom to think I wasted all the sugar. But even worse was the thought of going back to Food Giant. So I searched the cupboard and found something that looked exactly the same:

I measured out two cups and added it to the cookie batter. Then I refilled the empty sugar bag with salt.

Even I have to admit, that was pretty clever!

I think it's safe to say Mom will never know the difference.
Love,
PJ

132

PS. Mom just finished baking the cookies. We were all excited when she pulled them out of the oven because they smelled delicious!

But they tasted horrible!

I seriously don't know what happened.

Neither does Mom. She's taking another nap.

Chapter Eight
The Secret Laboratory Letter

MONDAY, APRIL 29

Dear Dad,

Mom wanted to throw away our gross cookies this morning, but I had a better idea.

It was still raining
during lunch. By now,
the plastic sheet
covering the hole in
the ceiling was full of
water.

It was hanging down
like a giant water balloon.

If you ask me, it looked
like a serious school safety
issue.

Where was Mr. Prince when we needed
him? Mr. Toots put up a
warning sign
and went
to find him.

DON'T
TOUCH
THAT!

↑
DANGER!

Ms. Julian set up all the shoebox dioramas today. She put them as far away from the hole in the ceiling as possible.

Everyone went over to check them out.

Of course all the girls liked Taylor M.'s the best. But only because it had a My Precious Pony in it.

Trust me, Dad. It was terrible.

Actually, they were all terrible. Mine was pretty much the only one that looked professional.

Well, mine and Benny's. Benny made a whole
Captain Big Boy scene, and it looked exactly like
the comic book! You could see Captain Big Boy, his
rocket ship, and even Professor No-Hair, who was
all burned up by the rocket ship flames. I don't
know how he did it, but it was pretty awesome!

After seeing that, I'm glad Ms. Julian didn't
make this a contest. Benny's would have probably
won.

Now that I think of it, I might redo mine as a Captain Big Boy diorama instead of a ninja one.

I told Benny that I was going to order Captain Big Boy's rocket from the comic book.

I asked him what the prize inside was.

But something told me he didn't even know about it.

Luckily, Dante changed the subject.

I showed Dante my list.

Just then, Mr. Prince walked in with his megaphone. He stood right under the giant water balloon.

Suddenly, there was a loud ripping sound.

It all happened so fast, I don't think
Mr. Prince knew
what hit him.

Mr. Toots came running in with a mop and a
bucket.

He was running so fast, he didn't even see the
giant puddle.

His legs started going crazy. Seriously, Dad. I've never seen anyone with moves like Mr. Toots's.

With a little more practice, he could do some incredible karate kicks.

He did a total flip . . .

. . . and landed right in his bucket!

I think Mr. Prince was mad because Mr. Toots totally stole the show.

Suddenly, Benny started jumping up and down.

Benny said he knew a secret about Mr. Prince.
A secret that nobody else knows!

Benny said he just pretends to run our school so he can commit crimes and the police won't suspect him.

HE'S NOT EVEN A **REAL** PRINCIPAL!

Mr. Prince is still mad that he didn't get to win the science fair when he was a kid.

THAT'S WHY **HE** STOLE THE ROCKET SCIENCE TROPHY!

I KNEW IT ALL ALONG!

Benny kept talking. He was making a lot of sense.

Benny was right. That trophy didn't belong to Mr. Prince. It belonged to us! I added his name to the list of suspects.

Benny said if Dante didn't believe him, he should look in the basement.

As soon as I heard that, I knew what we had to do.

As usual, Dante was scared. I guess you can't expect him to be heroic like me and Benny. After all, he's only a kid.

Benny led me to some stairs around the corner from Mr. Toots's closet.

First, I made sure my magnetic ninja pickle was still in my backpack. Then we went down. The door at the bottom was open a crack. There was a light on inside. I heard footsteps.

When I turned around, Benny was gone. I guess he's not always as heroic as he looks.

Luckily, I am. I sprang into action!

It was Sara!

She was standing by a huge shelf full of beakers and test tubes and other science stuff.

I couldn't believe it! Not only did I discover Mr. Prince's secret laboratory, but I discovered his secret assistant too!

I pointed my pickle at her. She was trapped!

The pickle sparked and flew out of my hands.

Sara ducked and it crashed into another shelf behind her.

It was full of trophies! There must have been a hundred of them. And I'll bet they were all stolen!

The trophy shelf wobbled . . .

. . . then it fell backward and crashed into the science shelf!

That's when Sara escaped!

On the bright side, at least none of the trophies broke.

I tried to pull my pickle free, but it was stuck to about five trophies. That's when I heard a voice coming down the hall.

It was Mr. Toots! I had to get out of there before he saw me! But how?

First, I turned off the light. Then I hid next to the door and waited until he came into the room.

When Mr. Toots walked past me, I ran! It was the perfect escape. Only one person saw me go.

I think it's pretty obvious I didn't really steal all those trophies. They were just stuck to my pickle. There was nothing else I could do!

I had to hide them where Sara couldn't find them. Luckily, I knew the perfect place.

It took all my strength to pull the trophies off the pickle. But I did! Now I just had to hide them.

As you know, sometimes the best hiding spot for a trophy is right out in the open. Sometimes people will think it just belongs there. Sometimes it can be right under their noses and they never even notice it.

As you can see, this was one of those times.

Just then Benny walked in.

I told Benny that he was right about Mr. Prince's secret laboratory. I also told him that Sara was his evil assistant.

As you know, I'm not just an incredible detective and an awesome ninja warrior, I'm also really good at coming up with plans. I took out some paper and a pencil and started to draw.

Here's what I drew:

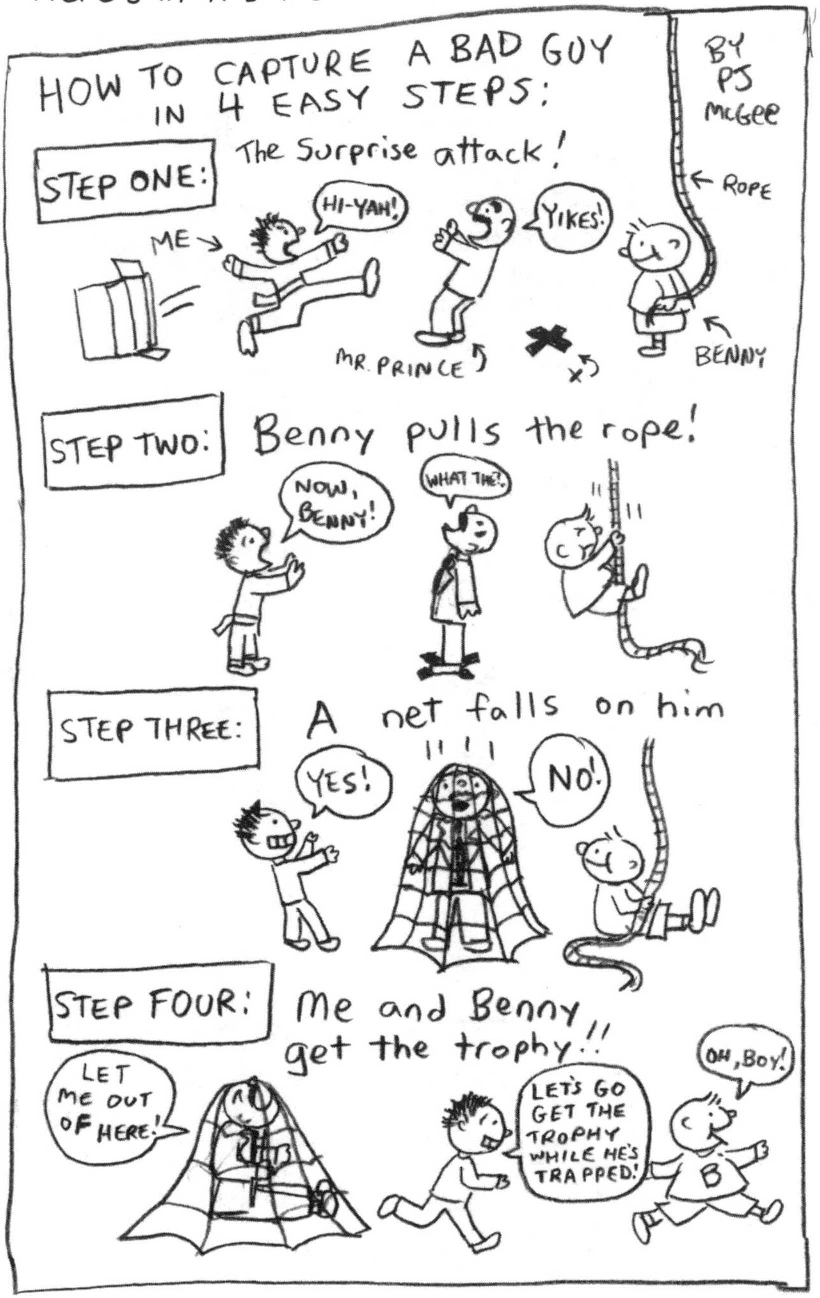
HOW TO CAPTURE A BAD GUY IN 4 EASY STEPS:
BY PJ McGee
STEP ONE:
The Surprise attack!
HI-YAH!
ME
YIKES!
ROPE
MR. PRINCE
X
BENNY
STEP TWO:
Benny pulls the rope!
NOW, BENNY!
WHAT THE?!
STEP THREE:
A net falls on him
YES!
NO!
STEP FOUR:
Me and Benny get the trophy!!
LET ME OUT OF HERE!
LET'S GO GET THE TROPHY WHILE HE'S TRAPPED!
OH, BOY!
B

This is definitely my best plan ever. It's so easy! Not only that, Benny says he has the perfect net for the job.

Tomorrow is the second meeting of Ninja Club. I think it's safe to say Mr. Prince will never see this coming! As you can see, Benny and I make a pretty good team. I just wish he'd remember to wash his hands more.

Love,
PJ

PS. I almost forgot to tell you: Right after I left the bathroom, I saw Mr. Prince talking to Mr. Toots. He was holding a broken test tube. And he looked mad!

I can't believe I ever thought he was a good guy. What a mistake!

I wish I never gave him your disco suit. *

Besides, he didn't even wear it once!

* SEE CLUELESS McGEE BOOK #1 PAGE 228. IT'S RAD!

Chapter Nine
The 2nd Ninja Club Letter

TUESDAY, APRIL 30

Dear Dad,

Today was the second Ninja Club meeting. I wanted to wear my ninja suit to school, but Mom said I couldn't.

PAJAMAS ARE **NOT** AN APPROPRIATE SCHOOL OUTFIT.

BUT I HAVE NINJA CLUB TODAY.

I decided not to tell her about my plan to capture Mr. Prince. Knowing her, she'd probably call that inappropriate too.

So I secretly wore my ninja suit under my new clothes. They were so big, Mom never even noticed!

When I got to the gym, Mr. Prince was hanging a giant sign above all the kick balls and hula hoops. Mr. Toots was trying to help.

While they were busy, I made an x-marks-the-spot on the floor with some tape. Then I took off my clothes and got ready for the battle of my life.

As you can see, Mr. Prince was already trying to fight dirty by taking away my ninja suit.

I looked around for Benny and his giant Captain Big Boy net. He wasn't here yet. Even though I was ready for our plan, I was getting a little nervous about him.

I got even more nervous when he finally showed up.

So while Mr. Prince gave a long boring speech about honor and respect, me and Benny planned a new sneak attack.

Dante sparred with Mr. Prince first.

Meanwhile, I hid behind a trash can.

Then it was
my turn.

I sprang into action with my scariest flying kick
ever!

Maybe it was even a little too scary.

As usual, capturing Mr. Prince was all up to me. So I did a reverse double-dagger spin flip . . .

. . . but I missed.

Luckily, Mr. Prince didn't.

He stepped right on the X and slipped on Benny's tiny net.

Then he fell backward into a pile of kick balls.

The kick balls bounced into the hula hoops, and the hula hoops went flying onto Mr. Prince.

Mr. Toots ran to help, but he tripped on his bucket. The bucket landed on Mr. Prince's head.

Then the safety sign fell on him. He was trapped! As you can see, my plan worked perfectly!

165

There was only one problem: Mr. Toots was there, so I couldn't make Mr. Prince hand over the trophy.

After Ninja Club, me and Dante found Benny's Captain Big Boy comic lying in the hall.

It looked like it had been read a bazillion times. It was all ripped up and falling apart.

I picked it up, but all the pages fell out.

Suddenly, I knew what Dante meant: This was the same comic book with Benny's booger on it! Except the booger wasn't on the comic . . .

. . . it was on my finger!

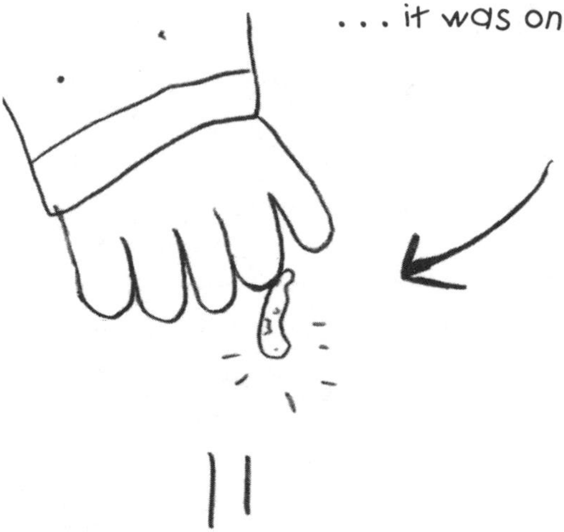

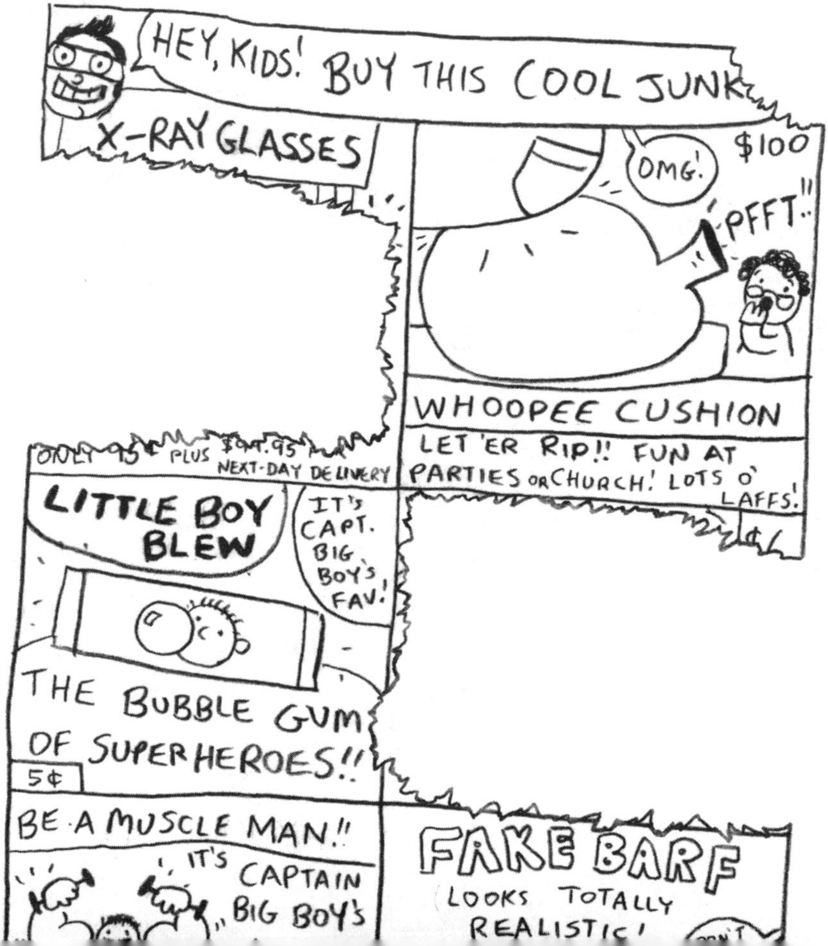
HEY, KIDS! BUY THIS COOL JUNK
X-RAY GLASSES
ONLY 95¢ PLUS $94.95 NEXT-DAY DELIVERY
OMG!
$100
PFFT!!
WHOOPEE CUSHION
LET 'ER RIP!! FUN AT PARTIES OR CHURCH! LOTS O' LAFFS!
LITTLE BOY BLEW
IT'S CAPT. BIG BOY'S FAV!
THE BUBBLE GUM OF SUPERHEROES!!
5¢
BE A MUSCLE MAN!!
IT'S CAPTAIN BIG BOY'S
FAKE BARF
LOOKS TOTALLY REALISTIC!

As usual, I tried to stay calm.

I looked around for something to wipe it on, but all
I could find was an old test tube lying in the corner.

So I used that.

How was I supposed to know the test tube belonged to Sara?

Me and Dante grabbed as many Captain Big Boy pages as we could. Dante got the page that had had the booger on it, and I got the rest.

When I got back to Mrs. Sikes's room, she made me put on my giant clothes.

She didn't even care that my ninja suit had just saved my life.

On the bright side, at least now I had a chance to read more of the comic.

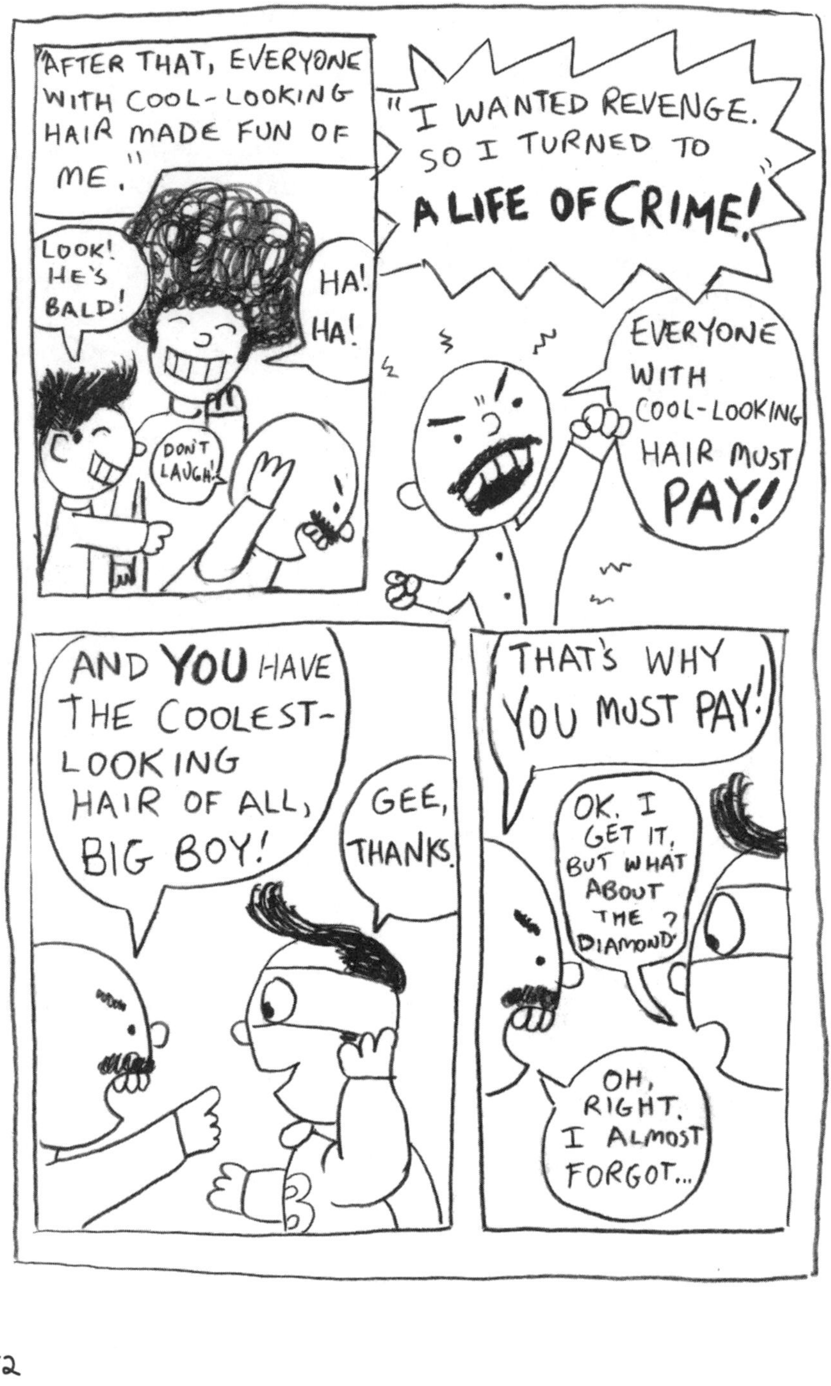
"AFTER THAT, EVERYONE WITH COOL-LOOKING HAIR MADE FUN OF ME."
LOOK! HE'S BALD!
HA! HA!
DON'T LAUGH!
"I WANTED REVENGE. SO I TURNED TO A LIFE OF CRIME!"
EVERYONE WITH COOL-LOOKING HAIR MUST PAY!
AND YOU HAVE THE COOLEST-LOOKING HAIR OF ALL, BIG BOY!
GEE, THANKS.
THAT'S WHY YOU MUST PAY!
OK. I GET IT. BUT WHAT ABOUT THE DIAMOND?
OH, RIGHT. I ALMOST FORGOT...

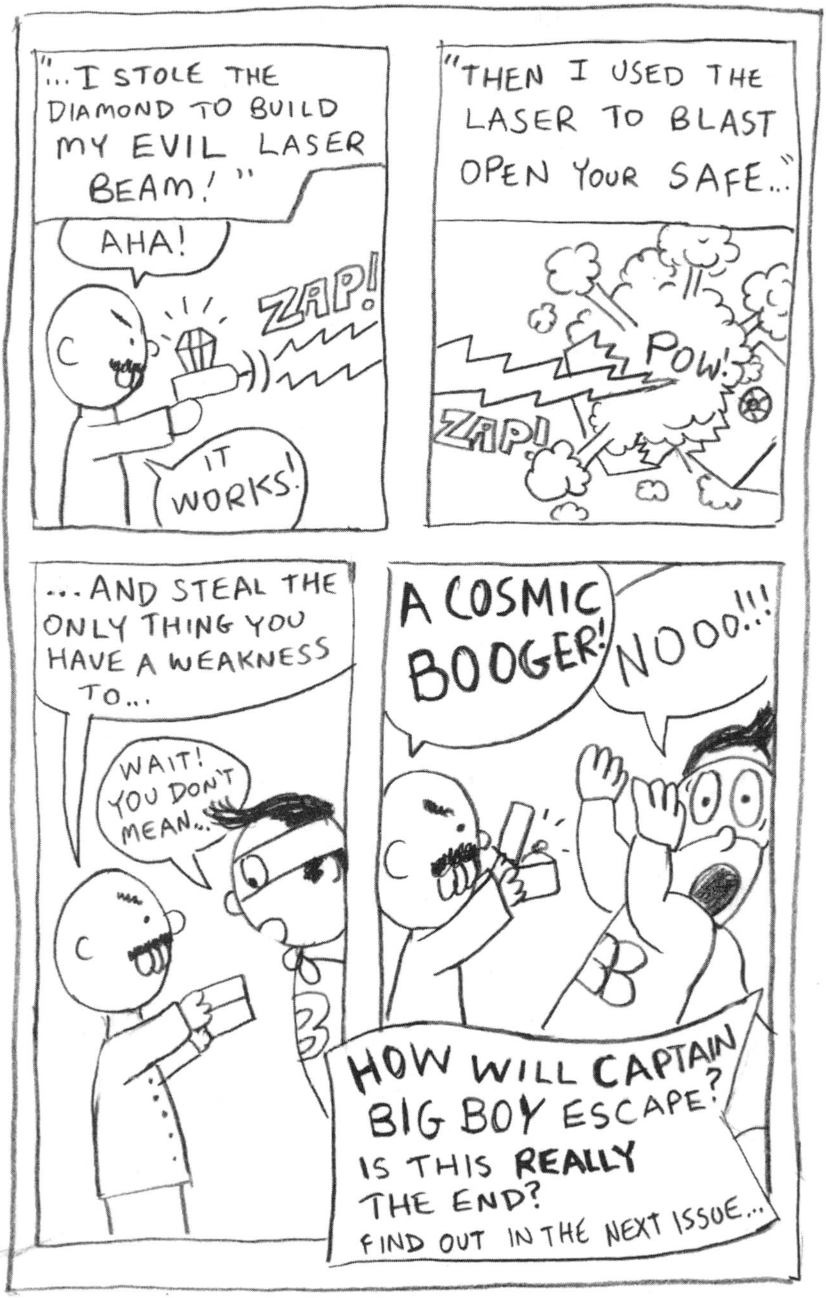
"...I STOLE THE DIAMOND TO BUILD MY EVIL LASER BEAM!"
AHA!
ZAP!
IT WORKS!
"THEN I USED THE LASER TO BLAST OPEN YOUR SAFE..."
POW!
ZAP!
...AND STEAL THE ONLY THING YOU HAVE A WEAKNESS TO...
WAIT! YOU DON'T MEAN...
A COSMIC BOOGER!
NOOO!!!
HOW WILL CAPTAIN BIG BOY ESCAPE?
IS THIS REALLY THE END?
FIND OUT IN THE NEXT ISSUE...

When I read the part about Professor No-Hair turning evil, I almost screamed. It was the exact same story that Benny told me about Mr. Prince!

They're practically the same guy! LOOK!

This proves that Mr. Prince is an evil scientist just like Professor No-Hair!

And it's all thanks to Captain Big Boy! He truly must be the greatest superhero ever!

I couldn't stop reading!

I was so excited, I thought of a brand-new hit single! I couldn't help it! I had to sing it out loud!

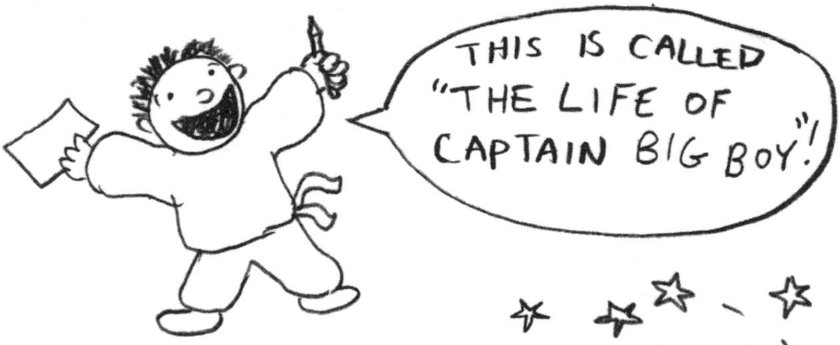
THIS IS CALLED "THE LIFE OF CAPTAIN BIG BOY"!

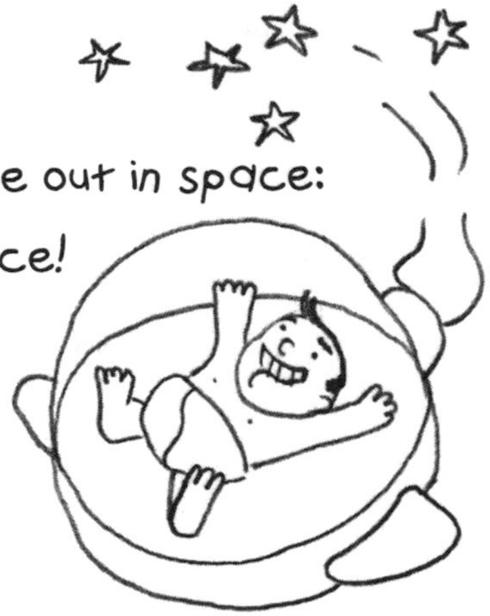

He came from somewhere out in space:
a baby with a big man's face!

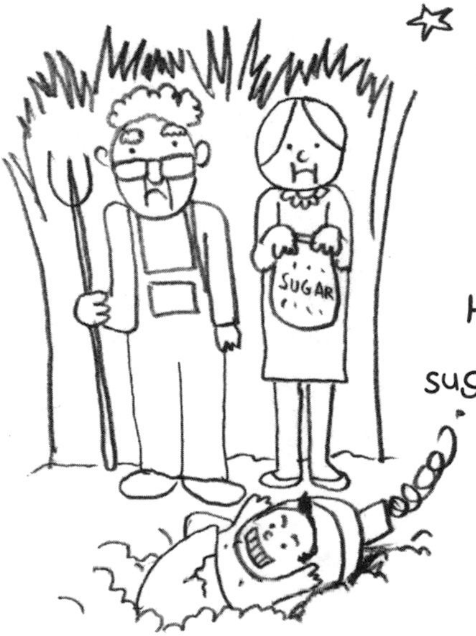
SUGAR

His parents owned a sugar farm.

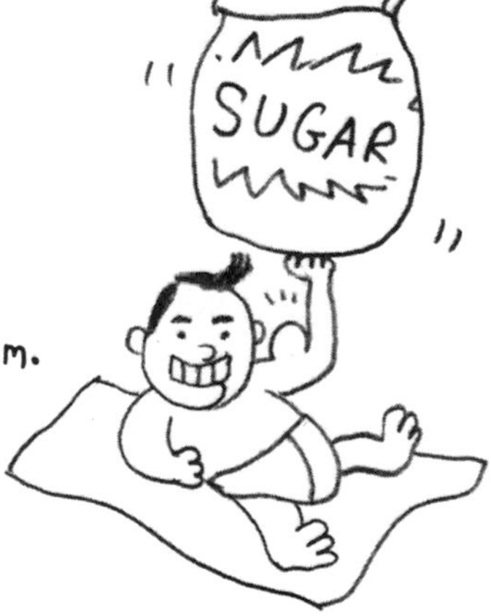
SUGAR

He grew a muscle in his arm.

The biggest muscles in his class.

His underpants filled up with gas!

He left the farm.

He left the sugar.

His weakness is a cosmic booger!

176

Now he's big.

He knows kung fu.
He chops the bad guys
black and blue.

HI-YAH!

His hair looks cool!

He wears a
cape!

MR. PRINCE
WILL **NOT**
ESCAPE!!

Mrs. Sikes took away my comic. She said it's a bad influence on the way I think.

But I don't think so.

Now that I think of it, Mrs. Sikes is probably one of Mr. Prince's evil assistants. Or maybe even an evil robot that he invented.

Only one thing's for sure: Mr. Prince must be stopped! And I came up with the perfect invention to do it:

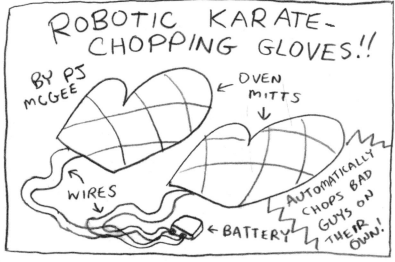

Once I figure out how to build these, Mr. Prince won't stand a chance! Then I can get the trophy back and save the day!

Love,

PJ

PS. I forgot to tell you: Something weird happened at lunch today. While me and Dante were eating, Benny came over and asked if we had seen his Captain Big Boy comic.

I told him that Mrs. Sikes stole it from me, but that Dante still had one page.

But Dante acted like he had never even seen it!

Even when I reminded him, he still pretended that he didn't know what I was talking about. It was weird. Plus, he kept winking at me.

If you ask me, Dante is just jealous that me and Benny are such awesome crime-fighting partners.

The whole time I was singing, Dante just sat there looking mad.

I don't know, Dad. I'm seriously starting to wonder if Dante is a good guy.

Something tells me maybe he's not.

Chapter Ten
The Robotic Karate-
Chopping Gloves
Letter

WEDNESDAY, MAY 1

Dear Dad,

I figured out how to make the robotic karate-chopping gloves last night. It was easy!

First, I distracted Mom with a smoke screen. (It was really just some flour!)

PJ!

FLOUR

PUFF!

HA! HA! HA!

Then I grabbed both of her oven mitts from the kitchen.

GOT THEM!

Next, I distracted Chloe with another smoke screen . . .

PUFF!

. . . and grabbed her talking parrot.

MOMMY!

Mommy! mommy! mommy!

I brought all of this stuff into my room and quietly closed the door.

Then I took the wings off of the parrot.

I tried to be careful, but I think something maybe broke inside, because now just the wing is talking.

I put one wing inside one of the oven mitts and the other wing inside the other oven mitt.

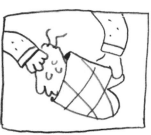

Then I tied all the extra wires together and hooked up the battery.

Mommy!

When I switched them on, the wings flapped and the gloves started chopping all on their own.

RZZZZZ!!!

EUREKA!

I still need to work on the controls, though. Sometimes the gloves go a little crazy.

RZZZZZ!!!

Mommy!

Mommy!!

mommy!

I brought them in to school today to show Dante. I figured he'd take one look at these and forget all about his horrible space-mail invention.

Suddenly, everyone wanted to check out my new robotic karate-chopping gloves! It was awesome!

That's when Dante and Benny got in a total tug-of-war over MY invention.

Now that I think of it, I probably should have told them to be more careful. Because while they were tugging, Dante accidentally pressed the "on" switch. At least, I think it was Dante. Anyway, the gloves went crazy . . .

. . . just as Mr. Prince walked into the room.

Mr. Prince dove under the table.

The gloves went chopping after him.

RZZZZ!!!

HELP!!

He tried to hide, but he couldn't get away! They were chopping like crazy, spanking him over and over!

RZZZ!!

MOMMY!
mommy!
mommy!

SMACK!
SMACK!
SMACK!

OW!
ow!
ow!

Finally, the battery ran out, and they stopped.

I couldn't see his face, but I had a feeling Mr. Prince was really mad.

By the time he finally stood up, Benny was gone. It was just me and Dante.

There was only one thing I could say.

It was no use. Mr. Prince sent both of us to his office anyway.

Luckily, I saw Benny on the way. And he gave me an awesome idea.

So, while we were waiting for Mr. Prince, I told Dante.

I thought it would cheer him up. But it didn't.

The trophy was way up on a high shelf. I knew there was a way to reach it, but as usual, I had to do it myself.

Just as I was about to grab the trophy, Mr. Prince walked in.

On the bright side, I think he believed me. But he still made me and Dante move our chairs.

Then he gave us a long boring lecture about how we should treat adults with more respect.

Not only that, he disqualified Dante from the science fair and gave me **ANOTHER** detention!

Dante was shocked. You could tell he was ready to freak out! I think I even saw a tear in his eye.

How does he ever hope to be my partner when he can't even stay cool under pressure like me?

Poor Dante. He really needs to get a grip.

Mr. Prince told Dante that he wanted to talk to me alone.

It sounded like a trap, but there was nothing I could do.

He said he was worried because I've been getting so many detentions lately. But seriously, Dad, whose fault is that? I wouldn't GET any detentions if Mr. Prince didn't GIVE them to me!

He said he was troubled by all the bad choices
I was making. As if battling evil scientists who
steal trophies from kids is a bad choice!

It was the oldest trick in the book: the bad
guy pretending to be my friend when he's really my
enemy!

I had to take a stand! I had to show this bad guy I meant business!

On second thought, maybe it was better if I pretended to join his team . . .

. . . for now.

Mr. Prince had one last word of advice before I left:

Benny was waiting for me outside.

I told him it was impossible while Mr. Prince was still guarding it.

As I was walking back to the cafeteria, I saw Dante standing by the trophy case. I have to say, I was glad to see him.

But he didn't seem very glad to see me.

I was shocked! I've never seen Dante get this mad in my entire life! There was only one thing to say:

After that, Dante didn't say anything. He just walked away.

So I guess I was right.

A couple seconds later, I saw Sara. She was yelling at some other girls. I didn't want to get involved, so I spied on her.

She sat down on the floor by the empty trophy case and started crying. Believe it or not, I actually felt bad for her.

As usual, I told her to look on the bright side.

Then again, maybe it was true. I couldn't think of a single person.

Sara went on. I sat down next to her.

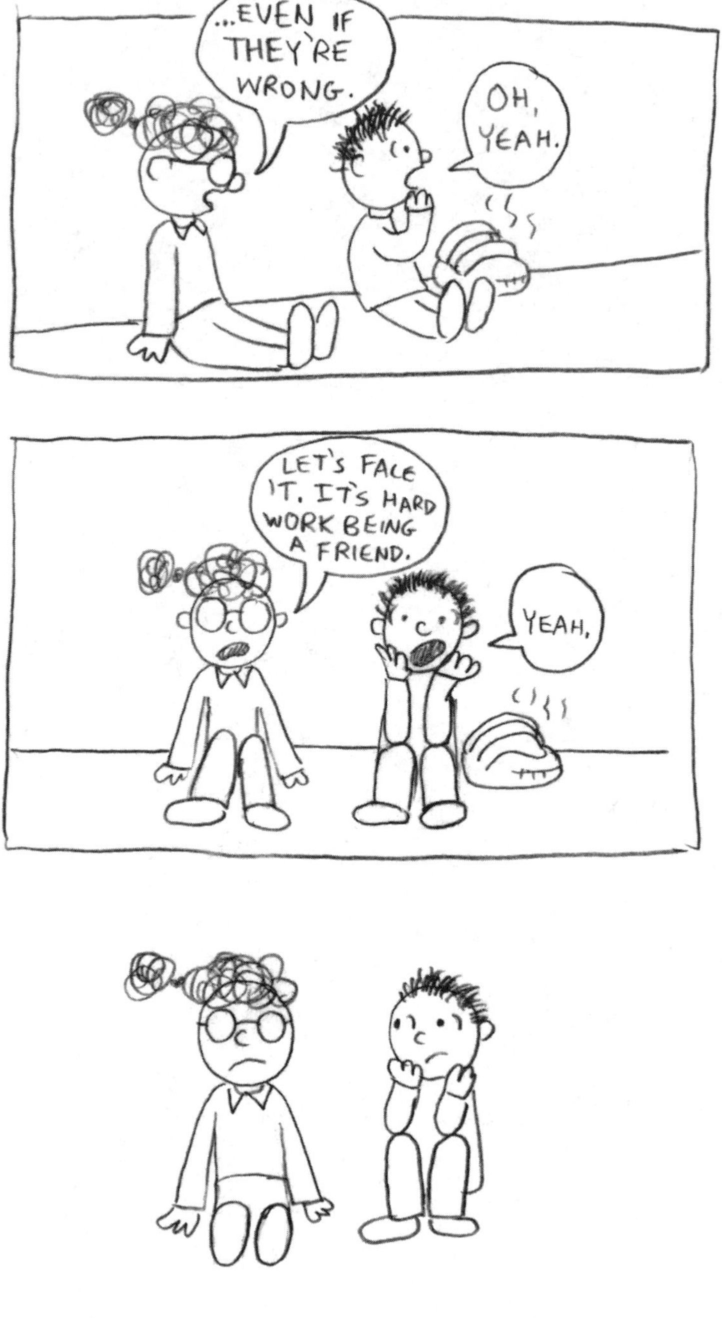
...EVEN IF THEY'RE WRONG.
OH, YEAH.
LET'S FACE IT. IT'S HARD WORK BEING A FRIEND.
YEAH.

Suddenly, I knew what I needed to say to Dante. I ran after him, but it was too late.

He was gone.

Not only that, when I went back to get my backpack, it was gone too! So was Sara!

What am I going to do, Dad? That backpack contains all of my plans and inventions! And now Sara's got it!

What if she and Mr. Prince form a team and use my inventions to take over the entire planet?

Or even worse, what if Dante doesn't want to be friends with me anymore?

I hope you get this letter soon, Dad. I really need your help! One thing's for sure: I can never tell Mom about any of this.

Love,
PJ

PS. Mom says I should apologize to Dante.

Chapter Eleven
The Science Fair Letter

THURSDAY, MAY 2

Dear Dad,

Today was the science fair. I knew there was going to be trouble, so I decided to wear my ninja suit. Except Mom washed it last night, and it shrunk. So now it's super tight on me.

On the bright side, it kind of makes me look like Captain Big Boy, don't you think?

YOU ARE **NOT** WEARING A CAPE TO SCHOOL!

BUT I HAVE TO SAVE THE DAY!

Luckily, I was able to hide it under my huge clothes.

At about ten o' clock, they called everyone down to the cafeteria for the science fair. Luckily, it wasn't raining, because Mr. Toots still hasn't fixed the hole in the ceiling.

Everyone was ready for science. Especially Mr. Prince! At first, I could only see the back of him, but it looked like he was dressed in some kind of sparkly science suit.

When he turned around, I almost screamed! He was wearing your disco suit! And everyone was staring at him!

PRETTY COOL, HUH?

I have to admit, he did look pretty cool!

When he saw me staring, he gave me a wink.

It's weird, but I started to think that maybe Mr. Prince wasn't such a bad guy after all. Let's face it: No bad guy has ever looked that cool!

When it was time to look at the inventions, Mrs. Sikes made everyone walk in single file around the room. The projects were on long tables, and there was a different inventor at each one.

They were all horrible. I didn't see a single laser beam or ninja weapon. Just a bunch of junk that no one can really use:

... a balloon that makes your hair stand up ...

a potato clock ...

some mold growing on a piece of bread ...

HEY! THAT'S MY LUNCH!

At least Ms. Julian left the dioramas up. I looked around to see who was admiring mine, but everyone was busy staring at the terrible science projects.

DOESN'T ANYONE CARE ABOUT ART?

When I got to the last inventor, I almost screamed again. It was Benny!

And his invention looked awfully familiar.

SPACE LETTERS

HELIUM

I couldn't believe it! It was the same as Dante's invention except he just changed "space mail" to "space letters."

BUT SPACE MAIL WAS DANTE'S IDEA!

DANTE GOT DISQUALIFIED. NOW IT'S MY CHANCE TO WIN!

It was time for Mr. Bellum to announce the winner.

Let me tell you, Dad, I was really mad! Dante was getting ripped off! I had to do something!

I grabbed the megaphone from Mr. Bellum.

I looked around the crowd for Dante, but he wasn't there. So I gave the megaphone back to Mr. Prince.

Suddenly, the door flew open. It was Dante!

Everyone gasped.

To prove it, Dante showed us the two ad pages. They both had the X-ray glasses ripped out . . .

. . . but Benny's had the rocket ship torn out too.

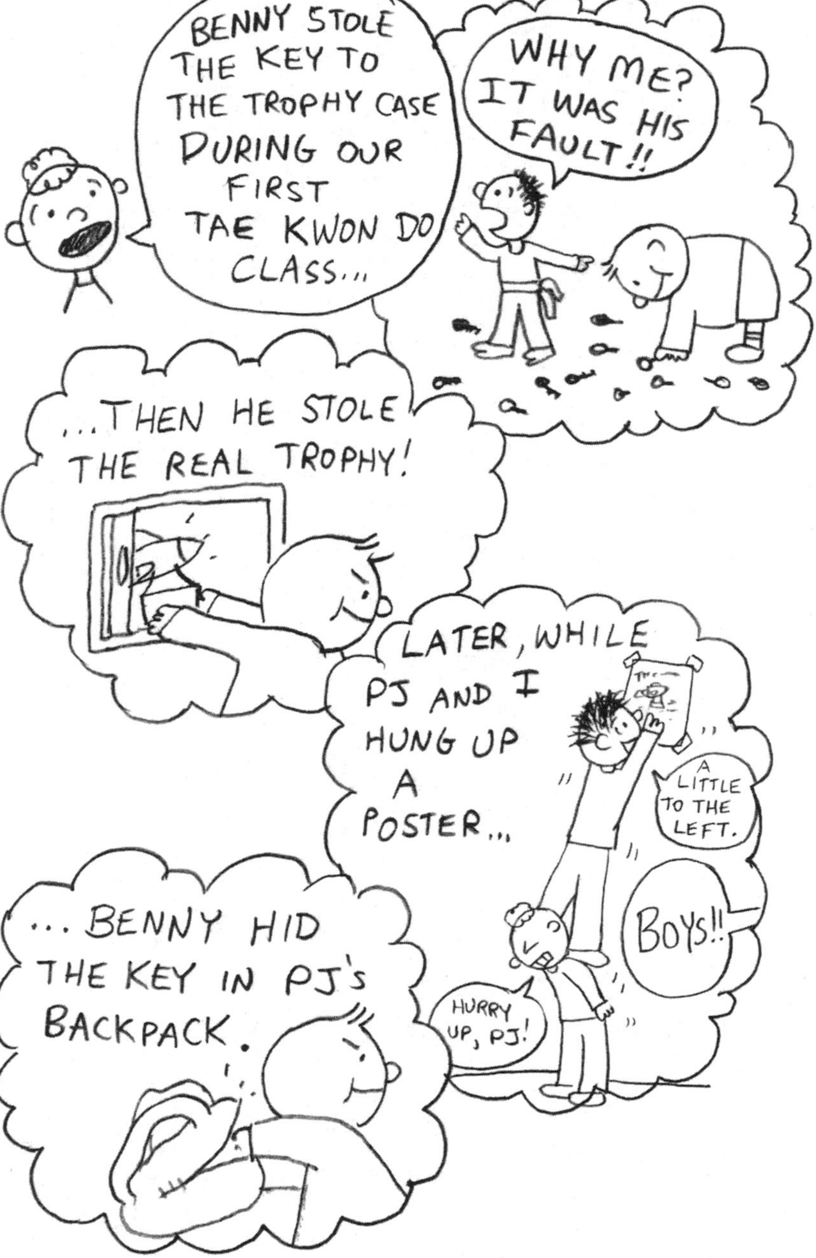
BENNY STOLE THE KEY TO THE TROPHY CASE DURING OUR FIRST TAE KWON DO CLASS...
WHY ME? IT WAS HIS FAULT!!
...THEN HE STOLE THE REAL TROPHY!
LATER, WHILE PJ AND I HUNG UP A POSTER...
A LITTLE TO THE LEFT.
BOYS!!
HURRY UP, PJ!
... BENNY HID THE KEY IN PJ'S BACKPACK.

A COUPLE DAYS AFTER THAT, HE HID THE FAKE TROPHY IN THERE TOO...
...JUST TO MAKE SURE EVERYONE THOUGHT PJ WAS THE THIEF!
BUT WHEN PJ TOLD HIM ABOUT THE SECRET PRIZE INSIDE THE FAKE TROPHY, HE WANTED TO GET IT BACK.
A PRIZE?! WHAT IS IT? IS IT A LASER BEAM? IS IT A UNICORN? WHERE DO BABIES COME FROM?
BENNY EVEN TRIED TO MAKE PJ THINK MR. PRINCE WAS AN EVIL SCIENTIST SO THAT PJ WOULD STEAL IT FOR HIM...
I WAS JUST DUSTING IT OFF.

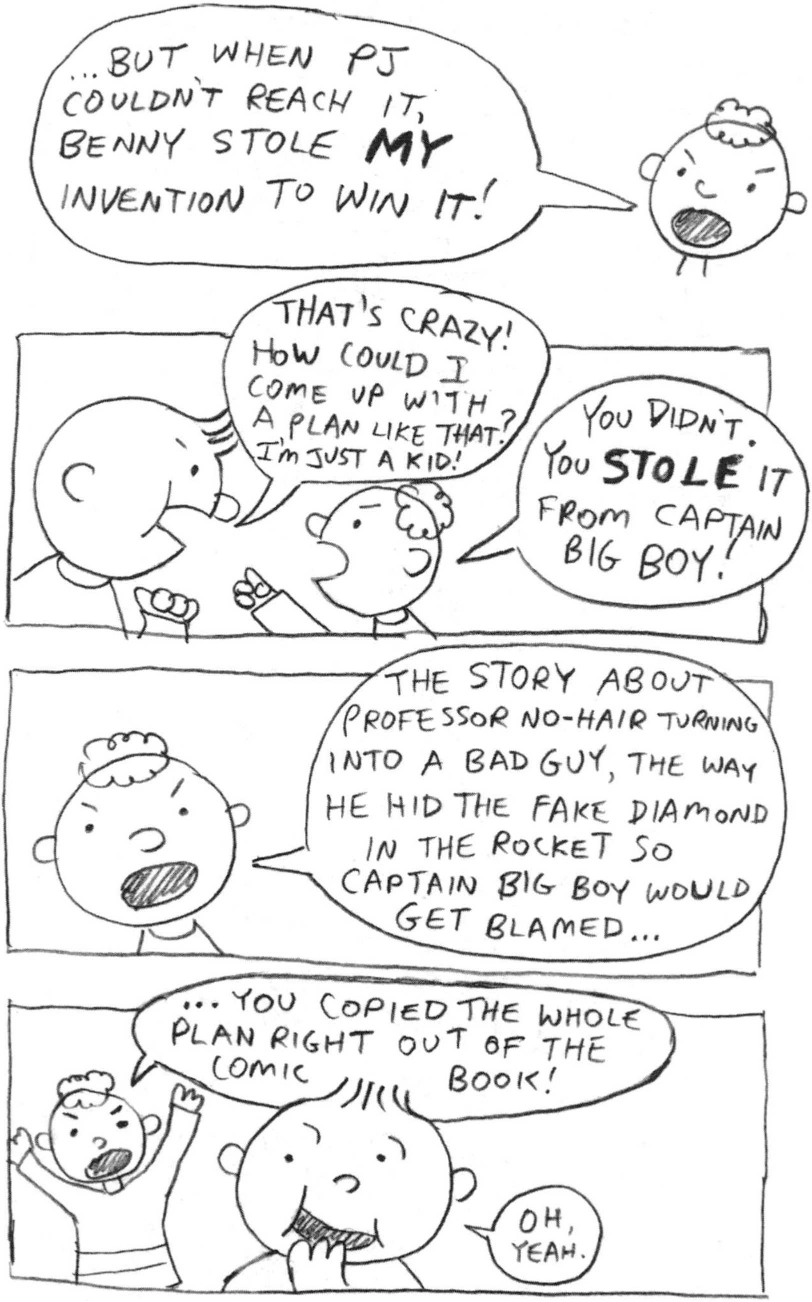
...BUT WHEN PJ COULDN'T REACH IT, BENNY STOLE **MY** INVENTION TO WIN IT!
THAT'S CRAZY! HOW COULD I COME UP WITH A PLAN LIKE THAT? I'M JUST A KID!
YOU DIDN'T. YOU **STOLE** IT FROM CAPTAIN BIG BOY!
THE STORY ABOUT PROFESSOR NO-HAIR TURNING INTO A BAD GUY, THE WAY HE HID THE FAKE DIAMOND IN THE ROCKET SO CAPTAIN BIG BOY WOULD GET BLAMED...
...YOU COPIED THE WHOLE PLAN RIGHT OUT OF THE COMIC BOOK!
OH, YEAH.

Mr. Prince looked kind of stunned.

Dante told me to take out my magnetic pickle.
There was only one problem: I didn't have it!

Benny was right! We had no proof!

He was going to get away with it!

That's when Sara walked in holding my
backpack!

She held the pickle up to the trophy in Benny's
hands.

It didn't stick.

RATS.

Mr. Prince took the trophy from Benny.

He looked at
the bottom.

Mr. Prince wanted to know where Benny hid the REAL trophy.
But Benny wouldn't talk.

Suddenly, the pickle started shaking and sparking!

It jumped up, flew across the room . . .

. . . and stuck right to Benny's diorama!

The real trophy was the rocket ship in the Captain Big Boy scene! It was right there in front of us the whole time!

Mr. Prince picked up the trophy from the diorama.

There was something on it. Something sticky.

He looked closer.

Mr. Prince
dropped the trophy
and ran.

But his foot got caught in the rope from
Benny's helium balloon.

The balloon went flying up.
And Mr. Prince went up with it!

He went straight through the hole in the ceiling, through the roof, and up into the sky!

Mrs. Sikes screamed!

Sara grabbed my arm.

She took a piece of paper out of my backpack. It was covered with drawings of my inventions. But they weren't my drawings. And it wasn't really my invention.

It was something totally different!

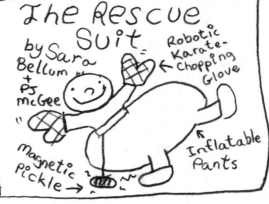

Sara explained:

It was true. They were all there: my magnetic pickle, my inflatable pants, even my robotic karate-chopping gloves!

Suddenly, it hit me. Not only was I wearing the perfect stretchy pants, I had an entire stretchy outfit on! I ripped off my clothes and showed her my ninja suit!

Sara put the new invention to work.

First, she tied a long rope around my ankle.

Then she used my ninja belt to tie the magnetic pickle around my stomach.

NOW PUT ON YOUR ROBOTIC KARATE-CHOPPING GLOVES.

OK.

Finally, she put the helium hose up my pajama leg and turned on the gas.

HISSSS

My whole ninja suit filled up like a balloon. I started to float up.

I went up through the hole in the ceiling. I turned on my chopping gloves, and they started to flap like bird wings. The next thing I knew, I was flying over the school!

Seriously, Dad!

I looked just like Captain Big Boy!

I could see Mr. Prince hanging from the space-mail balloon, his disco suit flapping in the breeze.

I used my robotic chopping gloves to steer toward him.

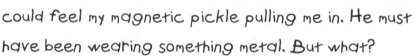

When I got closer, I could feel my magnetic pickle pulling me in. He must have been wearing something metal. But what?

I got even closer. But now I was going too high! I was losing control! The gloves were going crazy!

One of them accidentally chopped the balloon!

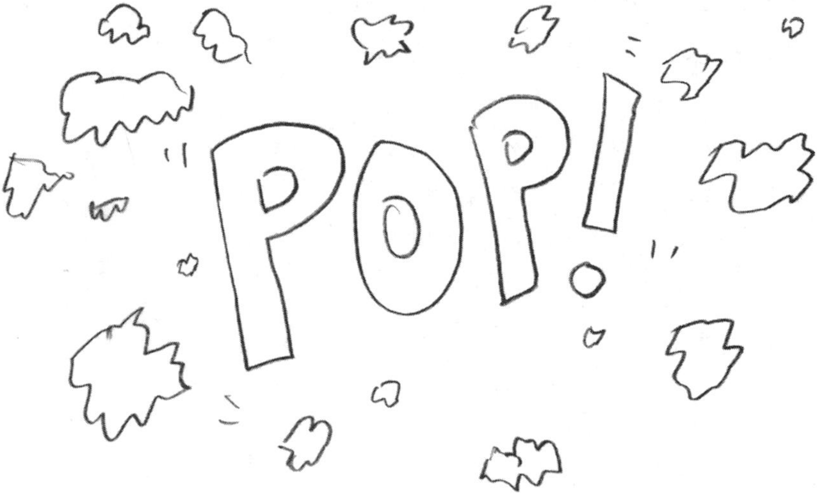
POP!

I closed my eyes. Was Mr. Prince a goner?

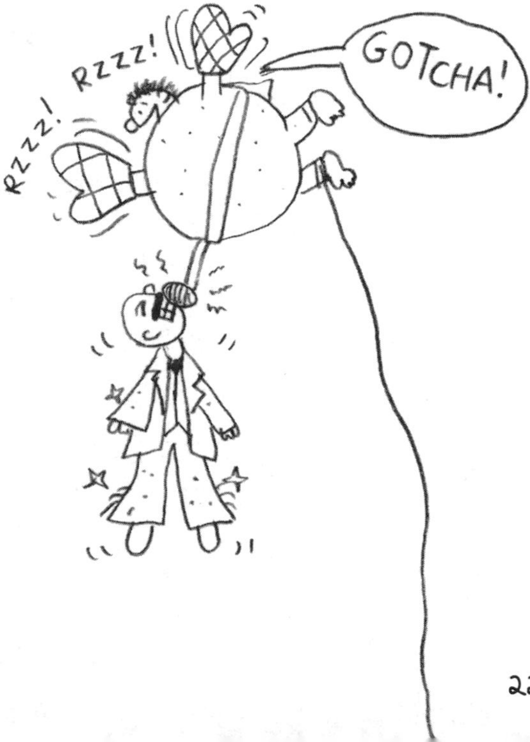
Rzzz!
Rzzz!
GOTCHA!

NO!

Just as he was about to fall, my magnetic pickle stuck right to his BRACES!

He was safe!

Sara started pulling on the rope around my ankle. Slowly, me and Mr. Prince sank back down to the ground. By then, we were pretty much safe.

When we landed, the whole fire department was waiting. Everyone started clapping and cheering for me! One of them said I was the bravest kid he'd ever met. Someone even took a picture of me and Sara for the newspaper!

Seriously, Dad. I could get used to being a hero!

Mr. Prince and Mr. Bellum decided to give the Rocket Science trophy to Sara because it was her idea to turn my inventions into a rescue machine. I think she'll be happy to complete her trophy collection once Mr. Toots cleans the booger off of it.

Even though they were really my inventions to begin with, I guess I'm glad she got the trophy.

Sometimes just knowing you've done a good job is enough reward.

Plus, I got all the applause!
    Love,
    PJ

PS. As you can probably guess, Benny was disqualified from the Science Fair. Mr. Prince made him go to the office and gave him TWO detentions! Plus, he left without taking his fake plastic rocket ship. You know, the one with the awesome secret prize inside?

Since Dante did sort of help me solve the mystery, I decided he should get the fake trophy and the prize. I looked around for him, but he was gone.

So I decided to open it myself.

Trust me, Dad. The prize was a total rip-off!

It figures.

Chapter Twelve
The Apology Letter

FRIDAY, MAY 3

Dear Dad,

What a week: Lying! Stealing! Telling! Let's face it, if there's one person at this school who deserves an apology, it's me. And I think Mr. Prince knew it.

Of course, saying you're sorry is never easy. It can be hard to find exactly the right words.

It wasn't much of an apology, but at least now the healing can begin.

That reminded me. I still owed Dante an apology. I looked for him during lunch. But he didn't show up. I have to say, it was a little boring eating all by myself.

Then I got an awesome idea.

This was probably the hardest poster I've ever made:

I just hope Dante realizes how much work this was!

Mrs. Sikes let me hang it up, even though it said frog-smacker. Let me tell you, it was embarrassing.

I don't know if the poster will make Dante want to be my friend again. But after all this trouble, he'd better at least read it.

Tonight after dinner, I put Mom's oven mitts back. I also tried to fix Chloe's parrot. I had to use a little tape, but I think I finally got it.

Since tomorrow is Saturday, Mom let me stay up late. I spent the whole time looking for the missing Captain Big Boy comic.

Just when it looked like I'd never find it, I found it! It was sitting right next to my bed!

Then Mom walked in carrying a big cardboard box. It looked like she was ready to throw my comic in the trash! There was no time to hide it!

There was only one thing left to do: beg!

And guess what? For once, it actually worked!

It turns out Mom had my comic the whole time. She was busy reading it! Can you believe that?

Mom dumped the cardboard box onto my bed. It was full of old comics!

What an incredible collection! There are twelve issues with Captain Big Boy, three with the Atomic Dentist, and eight with Green Lung-fish! Plus, some weird ones I've never even heard of.

Not only that, I'll bet they're worth a bazillion dollars!

Mom said she'd rather read them than sell them. She let me stay up an extra hour, and we read an entire Captain Big Boy comic together.

I have to say, it's a little weird reading comics with Mom. But it's still way better than baking.

Love,

PJ

Chapter Thirteen
The Bake Sale Letter

Dear Dad,

Our school had a bake sale today. So Mom and Chloe spent all day baking. They tried to make chocolate chip cookies again.

For some reason, the cookies took forever to bake. By the time they were done, we were late for the bake sale. As usual, Chloe was a pain.

The car ride to the school was scary. Mom drove like a lunatic!

By the time we got there, the bake sale was almost over. We had to get out of the car and run!

We were too late. The bake sale was over.

I didn't really feel like hanging out with Chloe and Mom right then. So I just wandered around a little. That's when I ran into Mr. Bellum and Sara.

For some reason, Sara was acting nice to me. It was weird.

Suddenly, I remembered! All that sugar I dumped down the sink! All that sugar that Mom thought she put in the cookies! It wasn't sugar at all . . .

It was salt!

I had to find Mom before she sold those cookies!

I couldn't believe it! Who on earth would buy such disgusting cookies?

I felt a tap on my shoulder.

It was Dante!

Dante was holding a piece of paper in his hand.

He handed me the poster, and I ripped it up.

And believe it or not, I actually sort of meant it.

Love,

PJ

Acknowledgments

Me and Jeff Mack have a lot in common: We both love to write and draw. Plus, when he was a kid, he used to build cool inventions like robots and

pinball machines out of cardboard boxes. I also heard he sometimes dressed up like a superhero or a sumo wrestler for no reason at all. Talk about embarrassing! If you want, you can visit him at www.jeffmack.com.

Some of his books are Frog and Fly, Good News Bad News, and The Things I Can Do. Some of mine are the first Clueless McGee book and this one.

Here are some people that I want to thank for it:

Mr. Green, my editor, who is smarter and funnier than ever. You rock, Mr. Green!

Ms. Megged and Mr. Steurer, who, like me, have incredible eyes for detail. They make sure my drawings aren't too messy and tell me anytime I mispell something.

Mr. Pfeffer, who is an expert agent. He said my next book should be worth a bazillion dollars! Can you believe it?!

Ms. Paluck, who is more than a friend—she's also a real-life editor! Plus, she is smart and nice and always doing stuff to help Jeff. Don't tell anyone, but I think he kind of likes her.

My friend Dillon, who isn't actually in this book, but who teaches me cool moves and tells the funniest stories ever!

Jeff's mom and dad, who, like I already said, are both really, really awesome!

Also, Jeff wants to thank his old art teacher Mr. Cole for staying after school and helping him paint that dinosaur mural even though he called Jeff "Mark" the whole time. Thanks, Mr. C.!

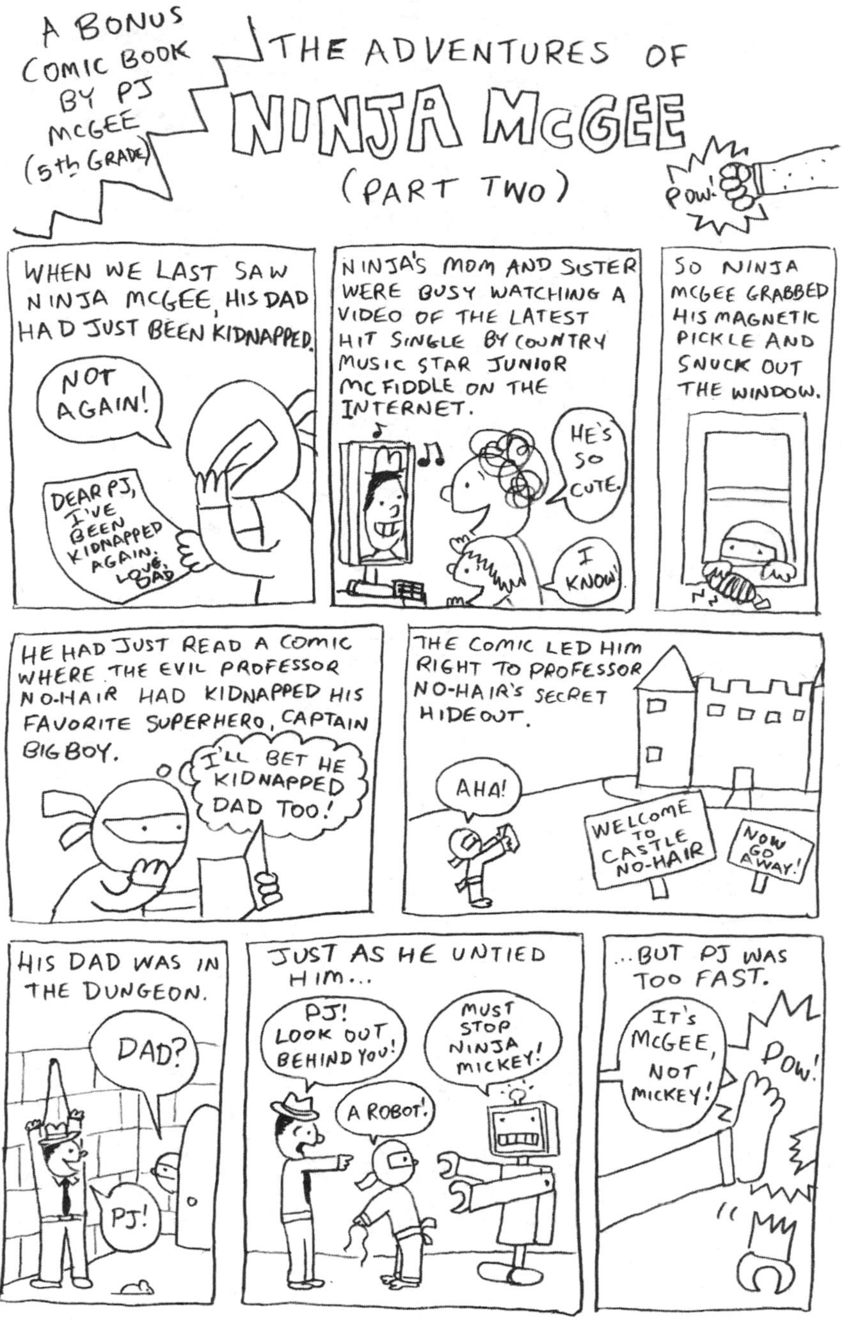
A BONUS COMIC BOOK BY PJ MCGEE (5th GRADE)
THE ADVENTURES OF
NINJA McGEE
(PART TWO)
POW!
WHEN WE LAST SAW NINJA MCGEE, HIS DAD HAD JUST BEEN KIDNAPPED.
NOT AGAIN!
DEAR PJ, I'VE BEEN KIDNAPPED AGAIN. LOVE, DAD
NINJA'S MOM AND SISTER WERE BUSY WATCHING A VIDEO OF THE LATEST HIT SINGLE BY COUNTRY MUSIC STAR JUNIOR MCFIDDLE ON THE INTERNET.
HE'S SO CUTE.
I KNOW!
SO NINJA MCGEE GRABBED HIS MAGNETIC PICKLE AND SNUCK OUT THE WINDOW.
HE HAD JUST READ A COMIC WHERE THE EVIL PROFESSOR NO-HAIR HAD KIDNAPPED HIS FAVORITE SUPERHERO, CAPTAIN BIG BOY.
I'LL BET HE KIDNAPPED DAD TOO!
THE COMIC LED HIM RIGHT TO PROFESSOR NO-HAIR'S SECRET HIDEOUT.
AHA!
WELCOME TO CASTLE NO-HAIR
NOW GO AWAY!
HIS DAD WAS IN THE DUNGEON.
DAD?
PJ!
JUST AS HE UNTIED HIM...
PJ! LOOK OUT BEHIND YOU!
MUST STOP NINJA MICKEY!
A ROBOT!
...BUT PJ WAS TOO FAST.
IT'S MCGEE, NOT MICKEY!
POW!

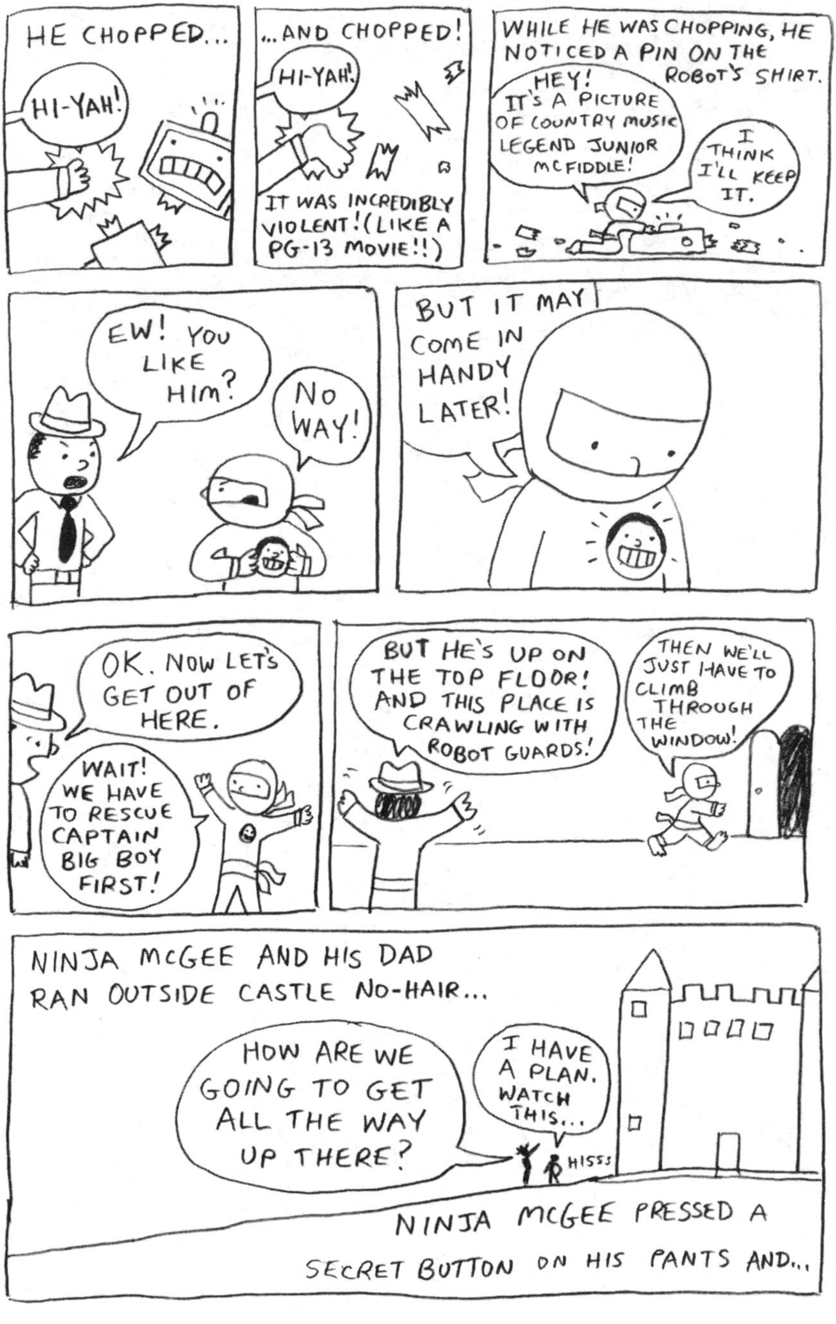
HE CHOPPED...
HI-YAH!
...AND CHOPPED!
HI-YAH!
IT WAS INCREDIBLY VIOLENT! (LIKE A PG-13 MOVIE!!)
WHILE HE WAS CHOPPING, HE NOTICED A PIN ON THE ROBOT'S SHIRT.
HEY! IT'S A PICTURE OF COUNTRY MUSIC LEGEND JUNIOR MCFIDDLE!
I THINK I'LL KEEP IT.
EW! YOU LIKE HIM?
NO WAY!
BUT IT MAY COME IN HANDY LATER!
OK. NOW LET'S GET OUT OF HERE.
WAIT! WE HAVE TO RESCUE CAPTAIN BIG BOY FIRST!
BUT HE'S UP ON THE TOP FLOOR! AND THIS PLACE IS CRAWLING WITH ROBOT GUARDS!
THEN WE'LL JUST HAVE TO CLIMB THROUGH THE WINDOW!
NINJA MCGEE AND HIS DAD RAN OUTSIDE CASTLE NO-HAIR...
HOW ARE WE GOING TO GET ALL THE WAY UP THERE?
I HAVE A PLAN. WATCH THIS...
HISSS
NINJA MCGEE PRESSED A SECRET BUTTON ON HIS PANTS AND...

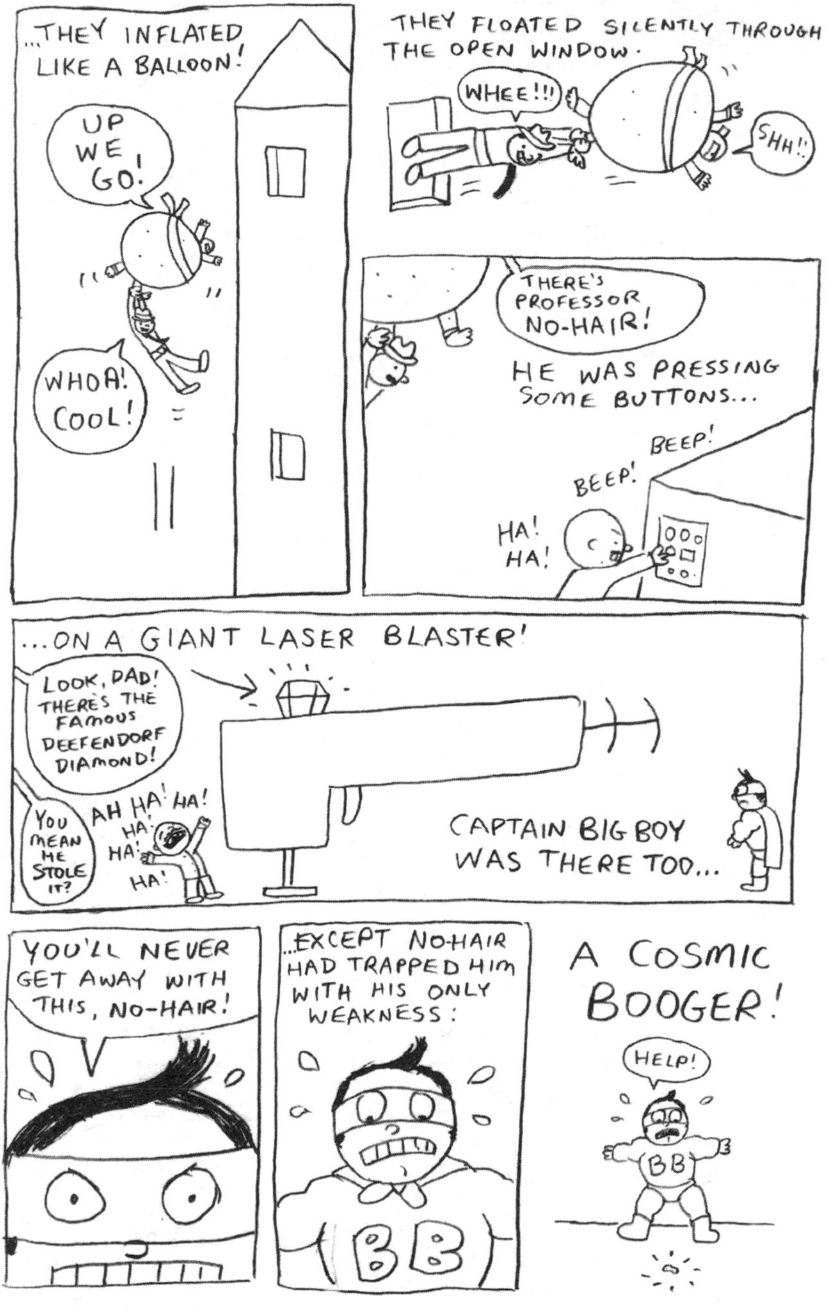
...THEY INFLATED LIKE A BALLOON!
UP WE GO!
WHOA! COOL!
THEY FLOATED SILENTLY THROUGH THE OPEN WINDOW.
WHEE!!!
SHH!!
THERE'S PROFESSOR NO-HAIR!
HE WAS PRESSING SOME BUTTONS...
BEEP!
BEEP!
HA! HA!
...ON A GIANT LASER BLASTER!
LOOK, DAD! THERE'S THE FAMOUS DEEFENDORF DIAMOND!
YOU MEAN HE STOLE IT?
AH HA! HA! HA! HA! HA!
CAPTAIN BIG BOY WAS THERE TOO...
YOU'LL NEVER GET AWAY WITH THIS, NO-HAIR!
...EXCEPT NO-HAIR HAD TRAPPED HIM WITH HIS ONLY WEAKNESS:
A COSMIC BOOGER!
HELP!
BB

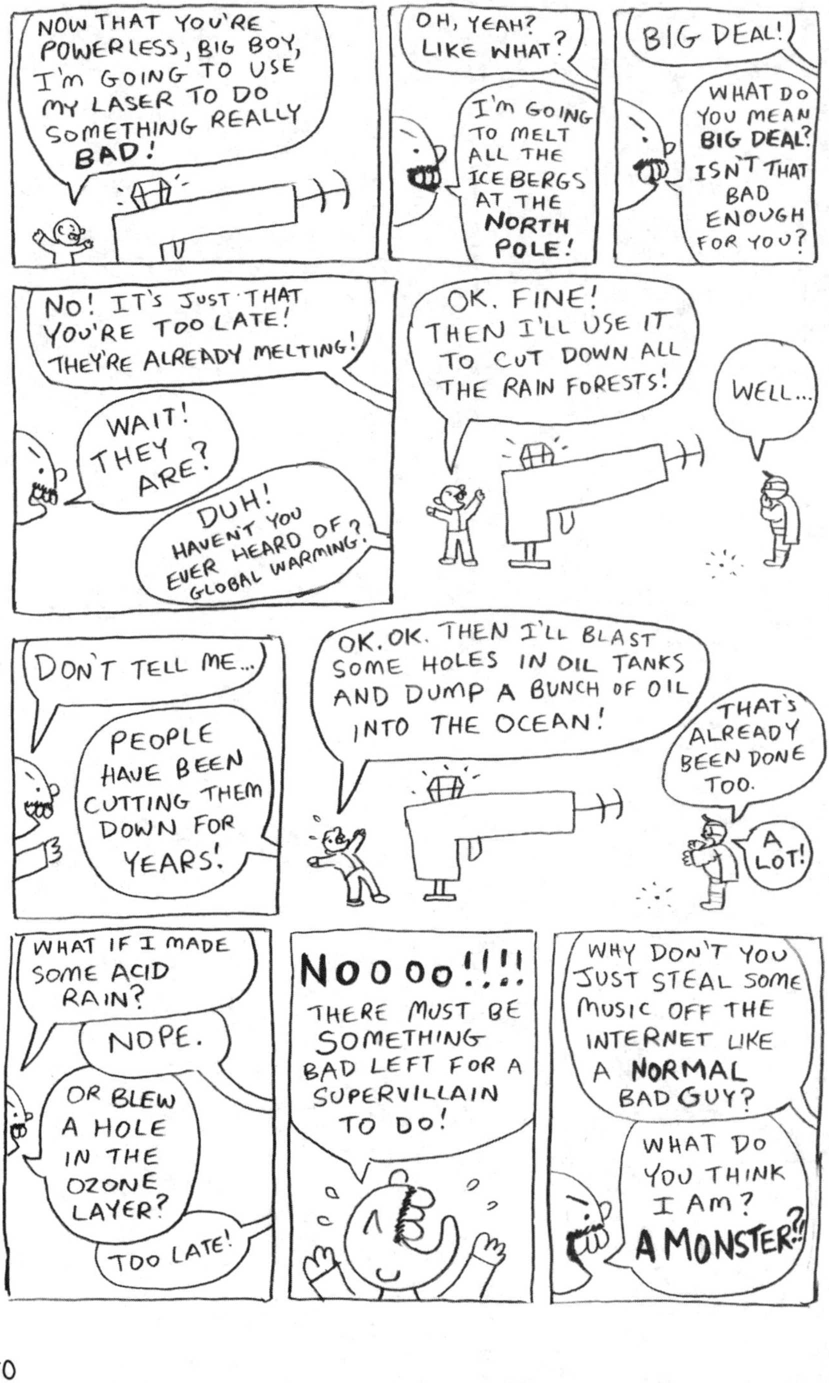
NOW THAT YOU'RE POWERLESS, BIG BOY, I'M GOING TO USE MY LASER TO DO SOMETHING REALLY BAD!
OH, YEAH? LIKE WHAT?
I'M GOING TO MELT ALL THE ICEBERGS AT THE NORTH POLE!
BIG DEAL!
WHAT DO YOU MEAN BIG DEAL? ISN'T THAT BAD ENOUGH FOR YOU?
NO! IT'S JUST THAT YOU'RE TOO LATE! THEY'RE ALREADY MELTING!
WAIT! THEY ARE?
DUH! HAVEN'T YOU EVER HEARD OF GLOBAL WARMING?
OK. FINE! THEN I'LL USE IT TO CUT DOWN ALL THE RAIN FORESTS!
WELL...
DON'T TELL ME...
PEOPLE HAVE BEEN CUTTING THEM DOWN FOR YEARS!
OK. OK. THEN I'LL BLAST SOME HOLES IN OIL TANKS AND DUMP A BUNCH OF OIL INTO THE OCEAN!
THAT'S ALREADY BEEN DONE TOO.
A LOT!
WHAT IF I MADE SOME ACID RAIN?
NOPE.
OR BLEW A HOLE IN THE OZONE LAYER?
TOO LATE!
NOOOO!!!! THERE MUST BE SOMETHING BAD LEFT FOR A SUPERVILLAIN TO DO!
WHY DON'T YOU JUST STEAL SOME MUSIC OFF THE INTERNET LIKE A NORMAL BAD GUY?
WHAT DO YOU THINK I AM? A MONSTER?!

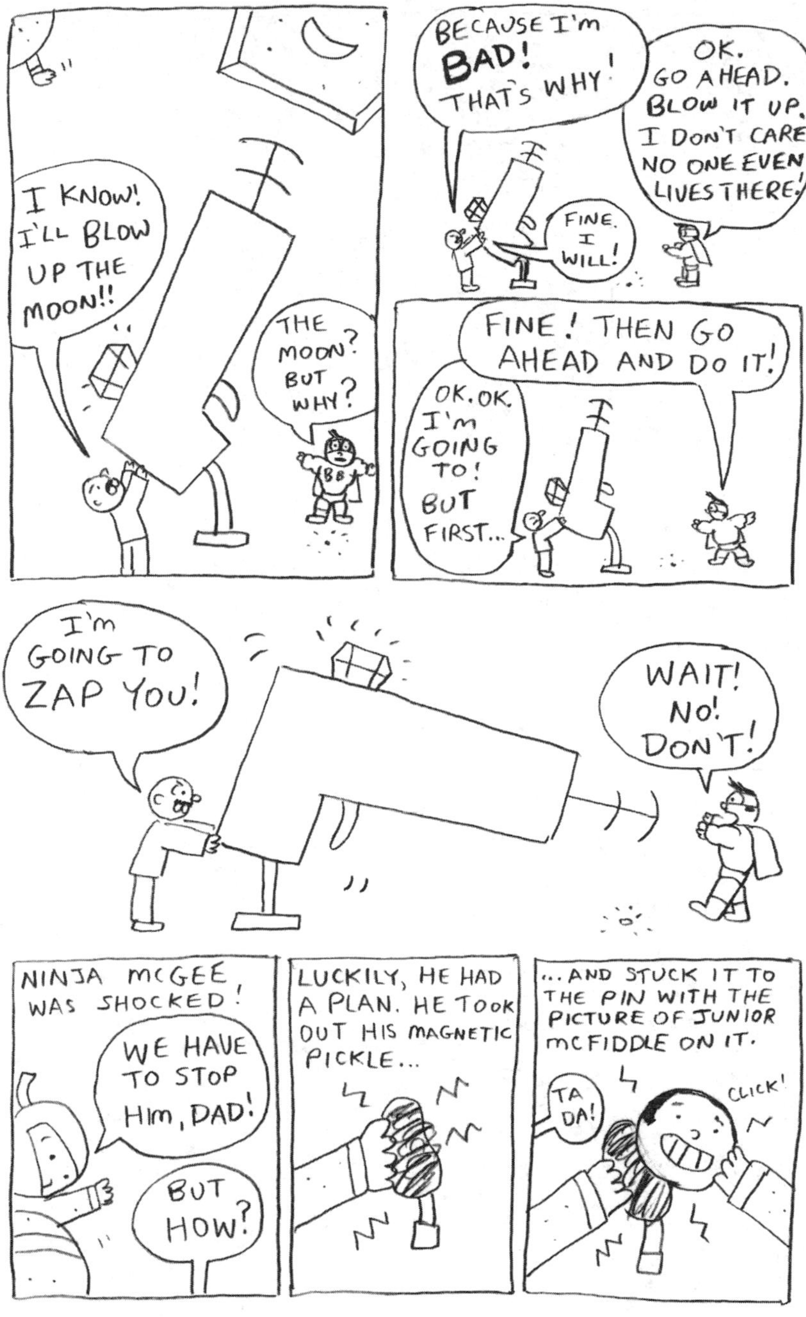
I KNOW! I'LL BLOW UP THE MOON!!
THE MOON? BUT WHY?
BECAUSE I'M BAD! THAT'S WHY!
OK. GO AHEAD. BLOW IT UP. I DON'T CARE. NO ONE EVEN LIVES THERE!
FINE. I WILL!
FINE! THEN GO AHEAD AND DO IT!
OK. OK. I'M GOING TO! BUT FIRST...
I'M GOING TO ZAP YOU!
WAIT! NO! DON'T!
NINJA MCGEE WAS SHOCKED!
WE HAVE TO STOP HIM, DAD!
BUT HOW?
LUCKILY, HE HAD A PLAN. HE TOOK OUT HIS MAGNETIC PICKLE...
...AND STUCK IT TO THE PIN WITH THE PICTURE OF JUNIOR MCFIDDLE ON IT.
TA DA!
CLICK!

THEN HE LOWERED IT ON THE ROPE THAT HIS DAD WAS TIED UP WITH.

JUST THEN, PROFESSOR NO-HAIR PRESSED THE LAST BUTTON ON HIS LASER.

FIRE!

CLICK!

ZAP!

WAS THIS THE END OF CAPTAIN BIG BOY?

NO! THE LASER BEAM BOUNCED OFF OF JUNIOR McFIDDLE'S FACE...

ARGHH!

ZAP!

...AND ZAPPED THE COSMIC BOOGER INSTEAD!

ZAP!

THE BOOGER BLASTED INTO A BAZILLION PIECES...

BOOM!

...AND SPLATTERED ALL OVER PROFESSOR NO-HAIR!

GROSS!

| CAPTAIN BIG BOY WAS SAFE! "I'M FREE!" "FREE AT LAST!" | HE GRABBED THE DEEFENDORF DIAMOND! "HEY! NO FAIR!" "I'LL TAKE THAT!" NOW THE BLASTER WAS USELESS... |

...SO ALL OF PROFESSOR NO-HAIR'S ROBOTS ATTACKED HIM INSTEAD!

"GO GET HIM!" "MUST" "STOP" "CAPTAIN" "BIG BOY!" "YIKES!"

BUT NINJA MCGEE AND HIS DAD KARATE CHOPPED THEM ALL IN LIKE FIVE SECONDS!

"THAT WAS EASY!" "HIGH FIVE, SON!"

| MEANWHILE, PROFESSOR NO-HAIR TRIED TO ESCAPE... HA! HA! HA! HA! | ...BUT THE POLICE ARRIVED JUST IN TIME! "HANDS UP, NO-HAIR!" "WHY? WHAT DID I DO?" | YOU'RE UNDER ARREST FOR STEALING JUNIOR MCFIDDLE'S LATEST HIT SINGLE OFF THE INTERNET! "RATS!" |

253

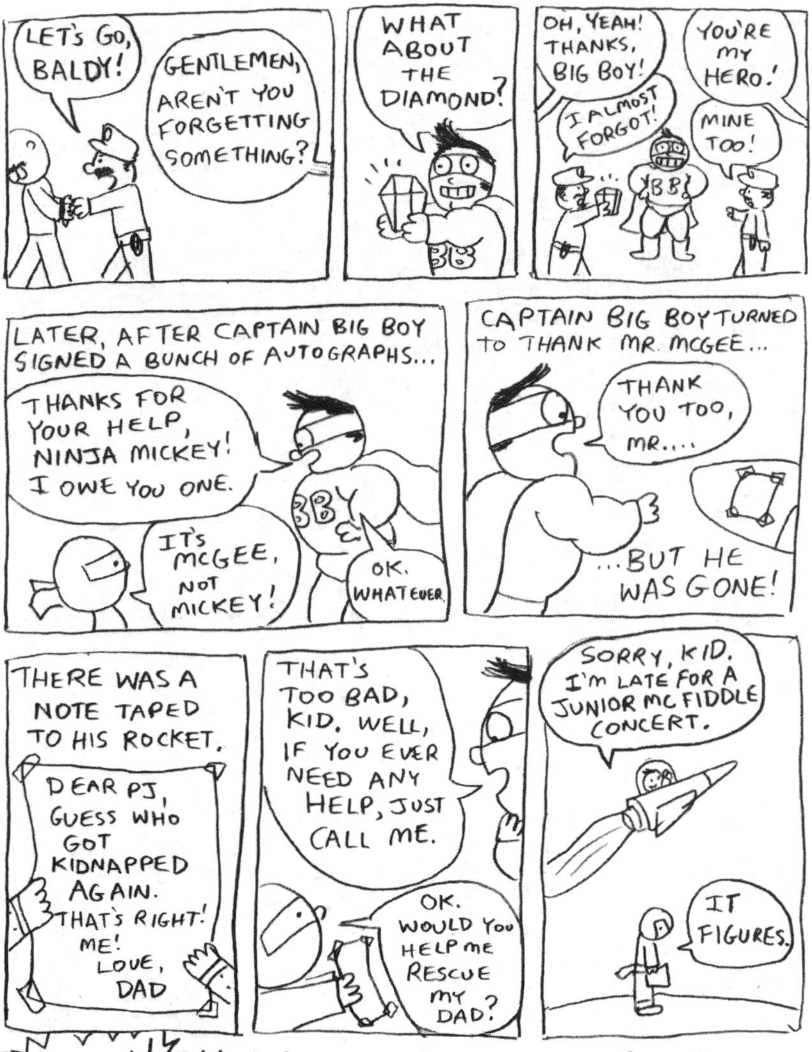
LET'S GO, BALDY!
GENTLEMEN, AREN'T YOU FORGETTING SOMETHING?
WHAT ABOUT THE DIAMOND?
OH, YEAH! THANKS, BIG BOY!
I ALMOST FORGOT!
YOU'RE MY HERO!
MINE TOO!
LATER, AFTER CAPTAIN BIG BOY SIGNED A BUNCH OF AUTOGRAPHS...
THANKS FOR YOUR HELP, NINJA MICKEY! I OWE YOU ONE.
IT'S MCGEE, NOT MICKEY!
OK. WHATEVER.
CAPTAIN BIG BOY TURNED TO THANK MR. MCGEE...
THANK YOU TOO, MR....
...BUT HE WAS GONE!
THERE WAS A NOTE TAPED TO HIS ROCKET.
DEAR PJ, GUESS WHO GOT KIDNAPPED AGAIN. THAT'S RIGHT! ME! LOVE, DAD
THAT'S TOO BAD, KID. WELL, IF YOU EVER NEED ANY HELP, JUST CALL ME.
OK. WOULD YOU HELP ME RESCUE MY DAD?
SORRY, KID. I'M LATE FOR A JUNIOR MCFIDDLE CONCERT.
IT FIGURES.

WOW! HOW IS NINJA MCGEE GOING TO SAVE HIS DAD NOW?

I GUESS YOU'LL JUST HAVE TO WAIT AND FIND OUT IN THE ADVENTURES OF NINJA MCGEE (PART THREE) COMING SOON!